Titia Sutherland was brought up in the country and has spent much of her adult life in London. She had a patchy education at various day-schools, and English was the only subject in which she received a good grounding. As a child she started many novels which were never completed, and she and her brother wrote and acted in their own plays. In her late teens she spent two years at the Webber-Douglas School of Drama and a short period in repertory before marrying a journalist. The birth of a baby put an end to acting. Following a divorce, she had a series of jobs which included working as a part-time reader for a publishing firm, and designing for an advertising agency.

She started to write when the children were more or less adult and following the death of her second husband. Her five previous novels, *The Fifth Summer*, *Out of the Shadows*, *Accomplice of Love*, *Running Away* and *A Friend of the Family*, are also published by Black Swan. She has four children, enjoys gardening and paints for pleasure when there is time.

AN
ACCIDENTAL LIFE

Titia Sutherland

BLACK SWAN

AN ACCIDENTAL LIFE
A BLACK SWAN BOOK : 0 552 99753 6

First publication in Great Britain

PRINTING HISTORY
Black Swan edition published 1997
Black Swan edition reprinted 1997
Black Swan edition reprinted 1998

Copyright © Titia Sutherland 1997

The right of Titia Sutherland to be identified as the author of this
work has been asserted in accordance with sections 77 and 78
of the Copyright Designs and Patents Act 1988.

Set in 11/13½pt Linotype Melior by
County Typesetters, Margate Kent

Black Swan Books are published by Transworld Publishers Ltd,
61–63 Uxbridge Road, London W5 5SA,
in Australia by Transworld Publishers (Australia) Pty Ltd,
15–25 Helles Avenue, Moorebank, NSW 2170
and in New Zealand by Transworld Publishers (NZ) Ltd,
3 William Pickering Drive, Albany, Auckland.

Reproduced, printed and bound in Great Britain by
Cox & Wyman Ltd, Reading, Berks.

For Diane with Love.

Grateful thanks to Roy Ward Baker
for his valuable advice on film production and direction.

Chapter 1

The shooting party had become a tradition, a friendly, informal affair which followed the same pattern each New Year's Day. It began at roughly eleven o'clock and drew to its end with the failing of the afternoon light and a gathering together of the participants. Guns were unloaded and flasks retrieved from pockets while the spoils of the day were counted and divided, the sound of male voices and sudden bursts of laughter echoing across the fields. Eventually the group would disband, and whistling their tired dogs to heel, drift slowly downhill to the cart track where the cars and the Land Rovers were parked.

On 1 January 1997 two men remained behind the others to take a last look at the winter landscape: rich brown plough patchworked together with grassland made emerald green from a month of constant rain. Against the downs, clumps of trees were outlined in black, skeletal detail, and over the lower reaches a ground mist was already rising, as theatrical as a Forties movie. Rooks flocked home to roost in the nearby woods, vociferously proclaiming the approach of evening. To the elder of the two men, Charles Stormont, the scene was a source of satisfaction and contentment; most of the land belonged to him, and it gave him endless pleasure to watch over it through the changing of the seasons. Glancing sideways at Philip

Stavely and about to speak, he was startled to see a look of such naked misery on the man's face that he turned away, embarrassed. The view, for all its stark beauty, could hardly be accountable for the expression, and there was no means of knowing what was going through Philip's head without questioning him. Perhaps he had had a tiff with Ellie. In any case, it was none of his business, Charles decided as he bent to pick up his game bag and sling it over his shoulder. Fond as he was of Philip, it could not be denied that he was given to swings of temperament, and the disquieting moment was dismissed quite easily from Charles's mind. Later, of course, he was to remember it with shocking clarity and blame himself for not acting on instinct.

'Give you a lift home?' he suggested.

'Thanks all the same, Charles, but I'd like the walk.' Philip smiled his famously sweet smile.

'Hope you enjoyed the day. I know blood sports aren't your cup of tea, but it was good to have you with us.'

'Likewise,' Philip lied politely, reminded of the carnage with distaste. It was his first experience of the shooting party. There were reasons for his being there, but enjoyment was not one of them. He tried not to think of the limp bodies of a rabbit and a pheasant looped together with string and dangling from his hand. 'The fresh air and exercise were much needed, in my case,' he added. 'I'm a couch potato by nature.'

'I never realized you were so proficient with a gun. Rather a pity shooting doesn't appeal to you. Where did you learn?'

'My father dragooned us into it as boys,' Philip replied drily. 'We didn't have much choice.' He looked up at the sky, a flat white expanse dusted with lemon yellow at the edges. 'Well, I suppose I'd better be on my way, it'll be getting dark in half an hour. Thanks again, Charles.'

'My pleasure. Give my love to Ellie.' Charles, his gun crooked over his arm, started downhill. 'By the way, I haven't heard a word from Dominic, have you?' he asked over his shoulder.

'No,' Philip called back, 'but I'd hardly expected to. He's on his honeymoon, after all.'

'I expect you're right. When they return we must get together, eh? Celebrate their homecoming.'

'Good idea,' Philip agreed mechanically, hearing his words ring out in false enthusiasm.

He watched Charles's tall, slightly stooped departing figure in its waxed jacket with affection; then he struck out across the fields towards the woods and the public footpath that led to home. He found it difficult to believe that a man of Charles's sensibility and intellect should have remained ignorant of his inner torment for so long. To Philip, it seemed each day of the last two years of leading a double life had been a showcase in which his feelings were on display for all to gawp at. He marvelled, with grim hindsight, that this nightmare had not become reality; that discretion and, it had to be admitted, his acting ability had prevented it, smoothing over countless moments of agonizing tension and imminent disaster. Deception had succeeded; the story had never broken, had avoided the ultimate shame of becoming sleaze fodder for the press. More remarkable, perhaps, was the unawareness of friends, even the closest of whom showed no sign of suspicion; rumours travelled fast and he would have been the first to learn of them. He had managed to keep his image

11

intact: in the eyes of all who knew him, he was Philip, married to the delightful Ellie with three children, actor, screenwriter and family man. Theirs had been reputed to be one of the few successful stage marriages, untouched by scandal. Ironically, it had survived the acting years; it was not until he had put them behind him that peace of mind had ended, with the advent of Dominic. The elaborate cover-up which ensued had taken its toll; he could see evidence of it each time he looked in a mirror, noticing a network of new lines and old ones scored deeper by the mouth and eyes. At times he felt tired beyond measure, unable to take the strain a moment longer. But what alternative had there been?

He had done it for Ellie's sake, and for the children's, this living a lie, to shield them from the unacceptable. That was how he had explained it to himself. In reality it was himself he had been protecting, unable to face the disgust in her eyes as he told her, terrified of losing her, and with her every vestige of stability. He wished, with a leadened sadness, that he had been able to conceal his feelings from her completely, and realizing that he had failed. It was their very closeness that had let him down: she had sensed the change in him, the reasons for which she could only guess at. Her unhappiness manifested itself in an uncharacteristic edginess and sudden silences in which she withdrew beyond reach. They knew each other too well, were too inextricably bound together by years of marriage for any sort of deviation to go unnoticed. He could but hope that she would never get to know the full story, and that if she did, she would come to understand. To forgive would be asking the impossible.

And now Dominic was gone, married to Clare:

sensible, uncomplicated Clare with her good classic clothes and her blinkered outlook. Gone with little warning or explanation, making a mockery of Philip's expended love.

He was reaching the end of the second field where the footpath ran alongside the woods. His boots were caked with mud from the day's walking, and each step felt heavy and in keeping with his desolation. He did not stop to scrape them on the rough grass, but kept on walking as far as the stile, and resting his gun against it carefully, turned to look back at the way he had come. He visualized himself at the centre of the field, neither here nor there but stranded in an open space symbolic of an emotional wasteland. There was no future for him; the knowledge did not come to him as a revelation. It had grown on him over the past weeks as he struggled with the hidden agony of Dominic's desertion. The loss of him was akin to bereavement. He imagined living with the pain within the family circle for the rest of his days, and found the prospect intolerable. He would never be able to make Ellie happy, to return to the way they were. She deserved more than the empty husk which was all that was left of him. Trapped in a situation from which he could find no escape, his brain had ceased to function in that miserable run up to Christmas. His complete aloneness had been the worst part, the impossibility of confiding in another living soul; although, if it had been otherwise, he would have chosen Cassandra whom he knew had guessed at the truth already. Cass, who silently absorbed with her eyes and seldom spoke of what she saw. He longed for the chance to explain to her, to make her understand that his transgression had been beyond his control and not of his choosing. But she was his child, and of course he had no right to burden her with confessions in an attempt to redeem himself.

Early on Christmas Day, during midnight mass, he had made up his mind as to what course he should follow. The idea had been there for some time, one of the few options open to him, lurking in the shadows of his consciousness. Only then, surrounded by flickering candles and the pungent smell of evergreen decorations, did he become blindingly certain that it was the obvious, the only solution. His decision brought an overwhelming sense of relief, so that at the end of the service he had managed to wish neighbours a happy Christmas and sound as if he meant it. Coming out into a still, cold night, Ellie had slipped her arm through his. 'You look much more cheerful,' she murmured. 'Are you feeling shriven?' Although it was lightly said, the question was near enough the mark to take him aback. He kissed her frozen cheek and made some banal remark in reply, horribly conscious that after all these years her happiness was still dependent on his own state of mind. In spite of the guilt he felt, he did not waver over his decision, but in the week between Christmas and the new year he put a great deal of effort into family relationships; trying to instil some confidence into the diffident Luke, helping Harriet with her new present of a puppet theatre, peeling vegetables for Ellie. He had not succeeded in getting through to Cassandra, who was brooding over the absence of her current boyfriend and refused to be drawn on the subject. Neither had he given Ellie that which she most needed, longed for and had a right to expect: the gift of being made love to; the one wish he was incapable of granting. But he had done his best, which was the least, as well as the most, he could give them in parting.

The daylight was fading now, and the sky had taken on the mauvish tint of semi-darkness. A single star hung there like a pendant; he did not know its name. An enormous calm crept over him, draining his mind of positive thought so that even the pain evaporated. His actions mechanical, he leaned over the stile and dropped the bodies of the pheasant and the rabbit on the opposite side. He would have liked to cover their stiffening corpses with dead leaves to give them the semblance of a burial; but the way he had planned the next, the final move made such a gesture imposs-ible. Then he climbed onto the step of the stile and straddled the wooden rail, lifting the gun after him. Facing him as he raised it and felt for the trigger were the lights of the village in the valley below, his home amongst them. They were the last thing he saw before falling headlong into darkness.

Ellie, who was preparing supper, heard the single shot as she stood at the kitchen sink. Poachers, she thought; the shooting party must have finished an hour ago; and she ran cold water into a saucepanful of carrots, half listening for the squeak of the garden gate heralding Philip's return.

Chapter 2

It had not crossed Ellie's mind that the press would take an interest in Philip's funeral. After all, it was a long time since he had appeared in the pages of a newspaper. Yet they were there on her arrival at the church, eight or ten of them huddled together like sheep against the cold with a couple of policemen firmly ensconced in front. They let Ellie pass in respectful silence on her way in; but after the service, as she led the small band of mourners from the churchyard with her brother-in-law Alex, several journalists broke rank and pushed close. There was a barrage of clicking cameras, and Ellie flinched as if she had been struck, tightening her grip on Alex's arm.

'How do you feel about your husband's death, Mrs Stavely?'

'How do you imagine she feels?' Alex said shortly, and using his considerable size, manoeuvred Ellie steadily forwards.

'Now then, move back, if you please,' the police admonished with outstretched arms.

Ellie looked anxiously over her shoulder for Cassandra and Luke who were following.

The voices persisted.

'Was your husband used to firearms?'

'Do you agree it was an accident?'

'Just a few words, Mrs Stavely.'

Alex raised his own voice above the others. 'Look,' he said, 'you're not getting a story because there isn't one. This is a private funeral and you are intruding on that privacy, so pack up and go home.' To Ellie he added, 'Go to the car, I'll wait for the children.'

But they were already emerging from behind the bobbing cameras, Luke white-faced and drawn, and Cassandra glaring from beneath her fringe.

'Piss off!' Ellie heard her say furiously.

Glancing back as she was unlocking the car, she saw the knot of reporters unravel itself and start to drift away, the remainder of the mourners presumably being of no importance. Trivial as she supposed the incident had been, she managed to scratch the paintwork with the key before Alex took it from her shaking hand.

'I'll drive,' he said, and helped her into the passenger seat solicitously, as though she were an invalid or decrepit.

'I'm sorry,' she said as they drove at a steady pace through the village. She felt an unnecessary need to apologize for her moment of panic.

Alex's left hand descended on both of hers where they lay inert in her lap, and squeezed them briefly.

'It was the unexpectedness of finding them there,' she continued. 'It's more than five years since Philip's last appearance as an actor. I didn't think of him as being newsworthy any longer.'

'The media has a long memory,' Alex replied. 'Practically every paper has included him in the past week, and he was mentioned on the television news. You may not have seen it,' he added gently.

She shook her head. 'No,' she said. 'No, I didn't.' How could she explain the almost total eclipse of her concentration in the days following Philip's death? 'Even so, I don't know what they hoped to gain from the funeral.'

'A story, as always. The circumstances are unusual, you see,' Alex said.

He means violent, Ellie thought; it was a violent death, and he is being tactful. 'I hope Cleo is coping all right with your parents and my mother,' she said quickly. 'It's kind of her to drive them.'

'It's the sort of thing she enjoys,' Alex answered, skirting the war memorial on the village green. 'You know how she loves to be thought indispensable.'

'Well, in this case she is.' Ellie's mouth twitched into the ghost of a smile. 'She's lent you to me for the afternoon, and I'm very grateful.'

'I would have driven the grannies and Grandpa if anyone had asked me,' Cassandra remarked in an aggrieved tone from the back seat.

'I know you would, darling,' Ellie said soothingly. 'They would have been rather squashed in the Mini, that's all. And what with Grandpa's arthritis—'

Her voice tailed away. She did so hope Cass was not going to continue her mood for long. There was the rest of the day to be got through: tea, drinks, hours before Ellie could seek the sanctuary of her bedroom and howl in peace. She knew quite well that Cass's barely suppressed anger was her way of combating grief, but that did not make her any less difficult. Lowering the small mirror in front of her, Ellie peered at her two children sitting behind her and staring out of the windows; Luke looked as if he might throw up at any minute. He had cried during the service, making no attempt to check the silent flow of tears; while Cass had sat dry-eyed, her fiercely clenched jawline the sole sign of emotion. Of the two temperaments, Ellie found Luke's unabashed misery the easier to handle: at least he was receptive to comfort, not having changed in that respect since he was small.

What a blessing you have the children, Alex's wife Cleo had told Ellie. They must be a great consolation and support for you. Only a childless woman would make such a sweeping statement, Ellie had said to herself in the midst of her pain. She would have hated to be without the family, but purveyors of moral support they were not, nor would she have expected them to be. Each of them, including herself, had to find his or her own method of living without Philip; even nine-year-old Harriet, who seemed to have a very tenuous grasp of what had happened. It was negative help that the three of them supplied, in that Ellie worried about them constantly, making it impossible for her to collapse for long in a sodden, despairing heap.

She had been alone in the house with Harriet on the evening of the accident. The police and Charles Stormont had broken the news to her only an hour and a half after she had reported Philip's absence, confirming what in her heart she already knew. Charles appeared to think himself responsible for Philip's death; she did not wholly understand why. They were kind and compassionate, but the blood in her veins seemed to have turned to ice and she could not respond. She wished they would leave, which they did eventually with reluctance, having failed to persuade her to call in a neighbour for company. 'Don't hesitate to ring if you need me,' Charles had told her, his face creased with anxiety. After they had left, she poured away the hot sweet tea brewed by a policewoman, substituted it with a whisky and prepared baked beans for Harriet's supper, going through the motions of a normal evening frozen in shock and moving like an automaton. The worst moment had been the explaining of Philip's accident to Harriet, the waiting for tears that strangely did not materialize. When at last she was on her own, Ellie had laid down on her bed and given way to a tide of weeping. She had not slept or even bothered to remove her clothes that night, and in the early morning she crept downstairs, made a mug of coffee and telephoned her mother. Through the window she could see a still, frosty day bathed in pale winter sunshine, and hated it for its tactless beauty.

After a while Harriet had joined her for breakfast and helped herself to cornflakes as though the morning were no different from any other. 'No,' she had said the night before when Ellie had talked to her of Philip's death. 'No,' she had repeated, shaking her head vigorously. 'I don't believe you; it's a mistake.' And she had gone to bed and to sleep without another sound. The sight of her daughter now, calmly spooning up cereal, completed Ellie's terrible loneliness.

'Darling, did you understand what I told you about Daddy?' she had said, unable to keep a note of sharpness from her voice.

Harriet nodded, lifting dark blue eyes to Ellie's tired face. 'You've been crying,' she remarked kindly.

She got down from the table and went to twine her arms round her mother's neck. 'Don't,' she said. 'He can't be dead. Daddy doesn't have accidents.'

Ellie, hugging her closely, whispered, 'He is, darling, he is.'

'Have you *seen* him dead?' Harriet asked.

Ellie shook her head wordlessly.

'Well then,' Harriet said as if that proved her theory, 'he'll come home: he's got to, I can't do the puppet theatre properly without him.'

From then on there had not been time to worry over Harriet's attitude. There were the funeral arrangements and the house was suddenly full of people: Ellie's mother, prepared to stay for as long as she was needed, and Cassandra and Luke, their new year celebrations cut short. And there was Alex, Philip's elder brother and trustee, who came and went between London and the house continuously, guiding, advising, organizing. Ellie found his presence infinitely soothing; later, when she suffered a mental blank concerning the ten days leading up to Philip's burial and could not recollect so much as the choosing of the hymns, she wondered how she would have managed without Alex. It was this same numbing of the senses that enabled her to survive the service and the lowering of the coffin into its resting place with some sort of dignity. The cold spell had lasted, and defying convention she wore the scarlet coat that Philip had given her for Christmas, modelled on a guardsman's greatcoat, for its warmth and because, whatever its unsuitability, he had chosen it. The prayers at an end, the vicar had closed his book and they stood in silence for a moment; Ellie had felt the wild desire to laugh which is a prelude to hysteria. Then she turned away and the little group followed her along the gravel path. She had caught sight of James Frobisher standing in the remotest corner of the churchyard, trying to look inconspicuous, and wished that she had issued him with an invitation to the service. Too late, she realized that his quiet support would have been infinitely welcome. Touched and surprised that he had bothered to be there, uninvited and remaining modestly in the background, Ellie had an impulse to ask him back to the house. But even as she thought about it, she saw his tall figure disappear from view through a side gate, and he was driven from her mind by the mob of reporters.

They had left the village behind them now, and were approaching the driveway to the house. The last ordeal of the day lay before Ellie, the plying of friends and relations with refreshments in the uneasy atmosphere that attended such occasions. No-one knew quite how to behave after funerals, she reflected; neither jollity nor gloom were in order. Those countries that celebrated death with a proper wake probably had the right idea. When this, the worst of days was over, she would have to start building a new life; there would be decisions to be made, the kind that she did not feel capable of facing, like whether or not to sell the house. Friends and acquaintances would be terribly kind, proffering conflicting advice and falling over themselves to have her to meals or to stay, making sure she was not alone. They had no means of knowing that she had lived with loneliness for the past two years; that something unexplained and disastrous had happened to her marriage and she had felt it crumbling around her, powerless to prevent it. Any attempt she had made to narrow the void between them had met with passive resistance on Philip's part, more wounding and frustrating than a downright admission of infidelity. For she could think of no reason other than an affair for the change in him. She had asked him once or twice, in the form of a hesitant query rather than an accusation: a plea for communication. He

22

denied it, just as he denied that a problem existed at all, retreating from her probing like a hermit crab into its shell. Defeated, she too had withdrawn and become, she suspected, a nastier person in the process, alternately snapping and sulking.

The house seemed to gaze at her benignly as Alex brought the car to a halt on the sweep of gravel, its windows catching the last of the watery sun. This was the house in which she and Philip had lived for the greater part of their married lives. The children had known no other home. They had been happy there, all of them, for most of the time, or so she had imagined. She was no longer certain of anything, with one exception: whoever had been the catalyst in the destruction of their marriage had not brought Philip happiness; the strain in his eyes had testified to some fierce internal battle which did not appear to have an outcome. He himself had decided its ending; of that she had no doubt, despite the official verdict of accidental death. They had shared so much over the years, and then at the last he had left her out in the cold. She was going to find it hard to forgive that final act of deliberate cruelty.

Cassandra, cruising round the sitting room with a plate of sandwiches in each hand, was stopped by her grandfather who was sitting in the high-backed armchair beside the fire.

'What's in 'em?' he asked suspiciously.

'This is egg and this lot's cucumber,' she answered, proffering the plates in turn.

He grunted and took two. 'What are you up to these days?' he questioned her with his mouth full. 'Left that university of yours yet?'

'Not until the autumn, after I've taken my finals.'

'Can't remember what you're reading.'

'Modern languages, Grandpa.'

'And where are they going to lead you?'

'Abroad, I hope. That's where I'd like to work.'

He gave a derisive snort. 'Funny sort of ambition; rather you than me.' He looked at her under eyebrows long and bristly as a prawn's tentacles. 'You never come to see us,' he complained. 'Too busy with your own life, I suppose, like all the young.'

'I will, I promise. In the spring.'

'This tea's gone cold,' he remarked, indicating the untouched cup on the table beside him.

'I'll get you some more. Or would you rather have a whisky?'

'I certainly would. Good girl,' he said, baring yellowing teeth in a smile of approval.

Cassandra discovered Luke talking to Cleo and gave him the plates of sandwiches. 'Your turn,' she said briefly. In the kitchen, she poured Grandpa Stavely's whisky. She alone positively liked her grandfather; the rest of the family thought him intimidating and ego-centric. A big man, tall and broad shouldered with an aqualine nose and iron-grey hair and moustache, he had scarcely altered with advancing age, apart from arthritis. His interests were limited to dogs, the Second World War, agriculture and rural sports, and he despised small talk. From conversations overheard in childhood, Cass had learned that Philip was a dis-appointment to his father. The stage as a profession was for poofters, according to Hugh Stavely, and his son's success did little to change his opinion. Cass realized he was a bully, but she had never been afraid of him; as the only reserved member of a demonstrative family, she could appreciate his dislike of outward displays of emotion. It was impossible to tell how, deep down, he was affected by Philip's death. Cass had seen him dabbing his eyes by the graveside, but that might have been due to the cold.

Betsy Groves, who had helped Ellie in the house for as long as Cass could remember, finished arranging chipolata sausages in a dish. 'Here, can you manage these, Cass?'

'I'll take Grandpa his drink first, then I'll come back for them.'

'How's your ma bearing up?'

'Don't know. All right, I think.'

Luke appeared in the doorway. 'Everyone wants a drink,' he announced. 'We'd better take a tray in.'

'OK,' Cass said. 'You see to it, then.'

'There's nowhere to put it.'

'The table by the window.'

'There's a bowl of flowers there.'

'Oh, for heaven's sake, move it,' Cass said irritably as she pushed past him, immediately regretting her impatience. He was not the cause of her ill-temper, merely the butt of it.

Snatches of conversation reached her as she passed round the chipolatas. Cleo, managing to look good in a hat like a coal scuttle, was questioning Ellie about Harriet's absence.

'I wonder,' she was saying, 'whether it was wise to send her away for today. She might feel excluded, don't you think?'

'If I thought that, I wouldn't have arranged it,' replied Ellie calmly. 'Have a sausage.'

'Thank you, dear.' Cleo gave Cass a brief smile. 'Well, of course, you know best,' she said to Ellie, 'but I

25

would have thought the chance for Harriet to say her last goodbyes – well, you know what I mean,' she added, gesturing perilously with a chipolata on a stick.

Cass admired her mother's self-control and moved over to where her two grandmothers were murmuring together. Granny Stavely had patched up the ravages of her tears in the bathroom with mauve powder and her face now looked like a damp violet. 'I was just saying to Fleur,' she told Cass, 'how wonderful of your mother to wear red. So brave, so defiant.'

'Yes, well, Daddy gave her that coat for Christmas,' Cass said. 'He hated black.' Her grandmother's huge eyes started to brim once more. 'Shall I get you a drink, Gran?' she asked quickly.

'A dry martini would be lovely, darling.'

'I'm not sure how to mix that. It's a cocktail isn't it?'

'Gin, darling, and just a whiff of the martini cork.'

'Shall I do it?' asked Ellie's mother, catching Cass's eye with amusement.

'It's all right, thanks, Granny. I'll manage.'

'Such a dear girl,' Cass heard Granny Stavely comment as she went in search of the drinks.

Cass did not see herself as lovable; her chief feeling was one of confusion, of a dozen different emotions pulling her this way and that. The death of her father was like a wound inside her that would not heal because she could not mourn him properly. A year ago she had inadvertently stumbled across a private part of his life which had shattered her faith in him; not her love, for that was not so easily destroyed. But the knowledge had inhibited her, making her awkward when they were together, and the warmth and closeness of their relationship was gone for ever. She had

26

waited and waited for him to talk to her about it, for some sort of explanation, but this had never happened, and now it was too late and she was left with nothing but regret and the pain that went with it.

She had not told her mother of her discovery; an innate sense of loyalty to Philip had prevented her. Hiding it from Ellie did not make her happy either: it was as though she were guilty of complicity, but it was impossible to be fair to both of them. The easiest way of dealing with the guilt, she found, was to shift the blame on to someone else, and her mother became the scapegoat, for no better reason than her calm acceptance of whatever life cared to fling at her. Her marriage had been in danger of disintegration; she might not have known the real cause, but she could not have been unaware of the fact, and yet she did nothing positive to save it. Or so it seemed to Cass from her position of unwilling observer. She had watched her parents withdraw from each other into their own private worlds. There were no arguments loud enough to be overheard. In the old days they used to have splendid and harmless rows over matters of no consequence that no-one took seriously and which ended in enjoyable rapprochement. But this was different; this was a drifting apart carried out in silence, which left an atmosphere heavy with unspoken reproaches. Cass, fretting under her secret knowledge, came home as little as possible. Each time she did so, she was amazed to find the situation unchanged. It was as if her mother did not want to know the truth and would rather suffer in ignorance; a sentiment so alien to Cass that it very nearly destroyed any sympathy she felt for Ellie, whose outward serenity infuriated her. Now Philip's death sat awkwardly between them, accepted as a tragic accident and unquestioned, just as his life had been unquestioned.

When most of the gathering had been supplied with drinks and conversation amongst them had become almost animated, Cass had it in mind to escape for a while, seized with a desire to speak to someone who did not belong to the family. Her mother, she could see, was talking to Dominic Fraser, erstwhile business partner and friend of Philip, and his new wife Clare. There had been a time, unbelievable as it seemed to Cass, when she had liked Dominic, had even secretly found him rather attractive. That was before her trust in Philip had been broken. Much of her thinking was divided into the before and after of that one moment, and now Dominic was associated with the worst kind of betrayal. Her aversion to him was such that she could hardly bear to exchange a few words with him, or to look him in the eye without her skin crawling. She had seen no reason why he should have been asked to the funeral, puzzling Ellie with her heated objections, and throughout the day had avoided him as far as possible. There was no way she was crossing the room now to join them; Ellie would have to manage without her for ten minutes or so.

In Ellie's room the bed was covered with guests' overcoats. Cass cleared a space and sat down by the telephone, her insides churning as they always did when she was about to contact Max. It did not happen often; he was married and disapproved of her ringing him at home. Sexual relationships between students and the faculty were severely frowned upon in any case; not that theirs had reached that stage as yet. Cass, who was agonizingly in love, liked to think of it as an affair, but realized in moments of honesty that it amounted to very little; a lift back to her lodgings one rainy night, dinner once or twice in an Indian restaurant, some wonderful but short-lived kissing in the car with the gear lever between them. She told herself that it was only lack of opportunity that prevented them from going to bed together. Max tutored her in Japanese, a langage with which she had genuine problems and a need for extra tuition. He took his work seriously; there was no messing around while he was teaching, and he bullied her when, absorbed in studying his bony, clever face, her concentration slipped. She told nobody of her infatuation, but it was not long before her peers had sniffed out the difference in her, including Paul, her boyfriend from her first university year. She had admitted nothing, but their friendship ended automatically through lack of enthusiasm on her part. Her closest girlfriend, having wormed the truth out of her, pointed out the craziness of falling for a married middle-aged man who was simply playing around. Cass, her common sense obliterated for the time being, ignored the warning and went blindly forwards towards an unknown goal.

Her mother knew nothing of this and merely attempted to sympathize over the split with Paul. Cass would have talked to Philip about Max at Christmas if it had been feasible; he rather than Ellie would have understood. But the gulf that now separated them had made it impossible. It never occurred to Cass to compare Philip's betrayal of Ellie with Max's cheating on his wife. There were a dozen excuses she could find to explain his seeking for experience outside marriage. He had more or less admitted that he and his wife were on different wavelengths; an intellect like his needed stimulus not to be found in the humdrum domesticity of everyday life. Nevertheless, she felt distinctly nervous as she lifted the receiver and dialled the number. It rang several times before a woman's voice answered against a background noise of small children.

'Hello?'

'May I speak to Max, please?' Cass asked meekly.

'I'm afraid he's in the bath,' his wife said cheerfully. 'Who is it speaking?'

'Cassandra Stavely. I'm one of his students, and I'm stuck on a piece of translation.'

'Oh dear. He won't be long. Shall I get him to ring you back?'

'No, thank you. I'll call him another time,' Cass said, losing her nerve completely. 'Sorry to have bothered you.'

'It's no trouble.'

She put the receiver to rest, her cheeks burning with shame at the niceness of Mrs Max Ehrhardt. The wronged wives of errant husbands had no right to be kind and obliging to the other woman; they should play by the rules. She realized that it had grown dark while she had been sitting there, and a crescent moon hung in a midnight-blue sky beyond the uncurtained windows. Everything about the day that was almost over, her father's funeral and the fact that both he and Max were in their separate ways unreachable, seemed to her suddenly and unbearably sad. The murmur of voices in the room below reminded her that she ought to be there, being supportive; she wished she were eight again, unwell and in bed while her mother cosseted her with mugs of hot milk, instead of rising twenty-one.

* * *

'What will happen to the partnership?' Ellie was asking Dominic. 'Will you find someone else?'

She forced herself to ask the question, knowing that if she did not face up to Philip's absence, she would hide from it for ever.

'It's very unlikely,' Dominic replied. 'It would be impossible to replace Philip. Collaborative writing isn't the same as other forms of team work; it's entirely dependent on minds running along the same lines. Phil and I—' he stared down at his glass, hesitating. 'We thought – and wrote – very much alike,' he said, clearing his throat. 'I can't imagine that happening with anyone else.'

He raised his eyes and Ellie was surprised to see they were glassy with tears. She had known him for three years, ever since he and Philip had joined forces as screenwriters. There were many ways in which she would have described Dominic – amusing, clever, confident, generous, and too smooth for her liking – but never sentimental.

'No, I expect you're right,' she said. 'It's exactly how I feel about marriage.'

He coloured up. 'I'm sorry, I didn't put that very well—'

'Nonsense. I believe you have a script in the pipeline. Will you finish it?'

'I shall try. Luckily it's three-quarters completed; we've already placed it.'

'That's good.' Ellie felt herself beginning to flag, overcome by the effort of appearing normal. To her relief Charles Stormont joined them saying, 'It's time we left you in peace, Ellie,' taking her hands and adding quietly, 'you've done splendidly.'

She saw them on their way from the front door,

Charles, his nephew Dominic and Dominic's wife Clare, whose cheerful cut-glass accents had dominated the muted hum of the afternoon's conversation incongruously. A strange marriage, but she had never considered Dominic as the marrying kind; she doubted he possessed the necessary tolerance. Their leaving was the cue for others to do the same. In Granny Stavely's case, getting ready was a long, drawn-out business; she mislaid her gloves, and saying goodbye to her daughter-in-law brought on a fresh bout of tears, while Hugh Stavely's patience was visibly stretched to breaking point. Eventually she was bundled into her ancient musquash coat (which she wore with a fine disregard for animal rights) and the sound of their car could be heard receding into the night. Finally the room emptied, leaving only Alex and Cleo and Ellie's mother Fleur Carrington, who was collecting glasses and putting them on a tray.

'I wish you wouldn't, Ma,' Ellie told her. 'Betsy and I will clear up later; it's all arranged.'

'I'm just going to put these in the kitchen,' Fleur said calmly. 'Take no notice. You don't need support with Alex and Cleo.'

Her serenity had the same irritating effect on her daughter as Ellie's similar attitude had on Cass. Ellie sighed, too tired to argue, and turned away to put another log on the fire. Alex was standing there alone, gazing at the flames, the light from them shining on his balding head.

'Will you be all right, Ellie?' he asked her.

She straightened up, dusting her hands, and pushed a lock of pale hair away from her forehead. 'Do you mean now, tonight, or in the future?' she said seriously.

'I really meant the present, when I – we – leave you, which we will have to do before long.' He looked searchingly at her face, white against the black of her polo-neck sweater. 'Do you have something to help you sleep?'

'Yes, but they seem to make me dream.' She was conscious of his presence, the solid dependability of him. 'I'll be all right,' she said. 'I've got Ma and Cass and Luke. But I shall miss you, Alex. I've grown used to leaning on you, that's the trouble.'

'You're not losing me,' he told her reassuringly. 'I'm on the end of a telephone, and besides, we are going to be meeting frequently while the estate is being wound up. It will entail your coming up and down to London quite often for the next few weeks. Would you rather I came here for discussions?'

'London, please,' she answered. 'I need to get away from home ground. What *am* I going to do with the house, Alex?'

'There's no need to decide now; you shouldn't make sudden decisions, there's time enough. I suppose I'd better nudge Cleo into fetching her coat,' he said. 'She's having a meaningful discussion with Luke by the looks of it.' He leaned down and gave Ellie a kiss on both cheeks. 'Try to rest; I'll call you tomorrow.'

'Yes, please,' she said. 'It will be something to look forward to.'

In the woodshed at the back of the house, Luke was refilling the log basket. His motive for undertaking the job was not entirely altruistic; the exodus of guests had left the hiatus he had been dreading, the moment when the family had to rely on each other for normal behaviour in an abnormal situation. It had struck him that, since no-one could possibly be hungry, it would be best to curtail the day by going straight to bed. Tomorrow, whatever happened, could not compete with today in awfulness. But he knew it was no use suggesting it; a kind of moral obligation to each other would force them to soldier on through another meal, searching for innocuous words. What the hell could they find to talk about? The funeral as a topic had been exhausted: the loveliness of the flowers, the choice of hymns, the vicar's address, the intrusion of the press. Any of the questions Luke wanted to ask, and there were plenty, would have to wait until Ellie was strong enough to listen. She, surely, must be querying at least some of the same things as he, like why Philip had joined the shoot in the first place when it wasn't his scene, and why he had climbed the stile without unloading his gun. Alternating with misery at his father's death, he felt a burning anger at the sheer carelessness of it. It was all so fucking unnecessary, Luke muttered under his breath while he dropped logs into the basket; as if Philip hadn't given a jot for any of them.

It wasn't just enigmas he wanted explained; he needed someone to talk to about his life, someone who would advise and direct and settle the qualms that increasingly attacked him. The year ahead was a crucial one; he was due to retake his A level maths, leave school and in the autumn join the Royal College of Music, studying piano and violin. Staying on simply because he had made a cock-up of the maths irked him; he already had top grade passes in both practical and theoretical music which were acceptable to the Royal College, but his mother had insisted. In the summer there was a possibility of backpacking round

India with a mate. It had been taken for granted by the family that he would make music his career; he went to a musically-orientated school and had not queried the blueprint of his future until six months ago. Then he had gradually come to realize that there were one or two of his contemporaries who showed outstanding talent and that he would never be included in that category; competent maybe, but without the spark that separated competence from brilliance. His teacher held the theory that talent could increase or decrease with time, and advised Luke to take his audition for the Royal College as planned. That had taken place in December and he had been accepted despite his deliberately careless performance, but he had lost faith in himself. He did not want to be second best, and somehow he had to tell Ellie how he felt, but the timing could hardly be worse. He should have explained it to his father at Christmas, when Philip had been in a particularly approachable mood; he would have understood Luke's predicament, having suffered agonies of self-doubt over his own career. But Luke had postponed raising the subject until after New Year, and by then it was too late. The only other person he could think of in whom to confide was James Frobisher. James had befriended him by chance when he was quite small, and they had had a special rapport ever since. He was also the best of listeners.

He did not know why he was finding difficulty in discussing things with his mother. It was not so much Philip's death that made it awkward, he decided, as the difference in gender, because it hadn't always been that way between them. In the growing-up years he had felt enormously close to her, just as Cass was closest to Philip, and Harriet, the afterthought, was everyone's darling. Luke had recently begun to find it easier to talk to people outside the immediate family; Cleo was a good example, he decided, remembering the conversation they had had that afternoon. They had discussed what he should see and do in India if he managed to get there, and then, as if they were two of the natural hazards of travel, she had switched topics to safe sex and drug abuse. Luke could not imagine mulling over either subject with Ellie, liberal-minded though she might be. Cleo talked easily, turning what might have become a lecture into an interesting exchange of views between adults, so that he felt older than his eighteen years. While they were speaking, he noted her features as if for the first time: the small aquiline nose, the hazel eyes and arched eyebrows, and skin the texture of thick cream, all faintly shadowed by the absurd but fashionable hat. With a shock of surprise, he had realized that she was attractive, even if she were an aunt by marriage and old enough to be his mother. For the short time they spent together, he had actually forgotten Philip, and Cleo had unknowingly bolstered his self-esteem which, never his strong point, had recently suffered a serious blow.

It had happened while he was staying with a school friend to see in the new year. There was an elder sister called Candida whom Luke had met before and hankered after ineffectually and without much hope. The three of them arrived home in the small hours from a local party, semi-inebriated and hopelessly giggly, and opened a further bottle of wine before finding their way unsteadily to bed. When Luke put his head on the pillow, the room rocked giddily behind closed eyes and he fell into uneasy sleep sitting upright. Sometime later – a minute or an hour, he could not tell – he was woken by a body slipping beneath the duvet beside him and warm arms wrapping themselves round him. Candida's scent drifted up his nostrils. Bemused as he was, he was conscious enough to realize that he was being offered the chance to lose his virginity and that he was not capable of doing so. The next fifteen minutes or so were best forgotten: a shaming mishmash of fumbling hands and tangled limbs, and a horrible sense of failure on his part as it became obvious that she knew what she was doing and he had very little idea. The next day, when they at last surfaced, she had made it plain that she held it against him by avoiding him as much as possible. Watching her drink cupfuls of black coffee at the kitchen table, her hair unbrushed and her face bare of make-up, he wondered what he had ever seen in her. The episode remained in his mind as a nightmarish experience, to such an extent that he had begun to question his sexuality and wonder if he were gay. He was supposed to stay for several days, but he was saved the embarassment by Ellie's telephone call sending for him, and everything else shrank into perspective with the news of Philip's accident.

The log basket had long been full; he could not hide in the woodshed for ever. Ellie was in the kitchen stacking the dishwasher with teacups and glasses as he struggled through the back door. She straightened up and smiled at him; her face translucent with tiredness.

'Cass has gone to get some pizzas and a video,' she told him. 'I thought we'd eat in front of the television. I don't think any of us feels like talking; we've done enough of it for today.'

Luke felt a rush of affection for her. 'Brilliant,' he said in relief. 'I'll go and make up the fire, shall I?'

'Don't mind me if you want to cry,' Harriet's friend Flora said in the darkness of her bedroom. 'I'll pretend not to notice.'

'I don't want to, thanks. Why should I?' Harriet answered.

'Well, *I* would if my father died. .Bother! I wasn't meant to say anything about it. Mummy said it might upset you, but it's difficult to remember when you seem really cheerful to me.'

'That's because I like staying here, and anyway, Daddy isn't dead,' Harriet said. 'He's only disappeared. Mum's sad because he didn't leave a note saying why he'd gone, so *she* thinks he's dead. It's all a huge mistake.'

'But what about the funeral?' Flora sounded thoroughly puzzled.

Harriet did not answer immediately; she was rather uncertain about the funeral. If she thought hard enough an explanation would probably come to her. She turned her head on the pillow; in the next-door bed Flora's face showed up palely in the semi-darkness.

'I don't think there's actually been a funeral,' Harriet stated on the spur of the moment. 'I think Mum just pretended there was going to be one', she went on, 'so that I would believe about Daddy's accident and stop asking questions. It was supposed to be a family funeral, and that means *I* would have been there if it had happened.'

'Grown-ups don't make things up as a rule,' Flora commented doubtfully. 'Anyway, why would your father disappear? Where would he go to?'

'I can think of lots of reasons; it just depends which one it is.' Harriet felt on safer ground; inventing things presented no problem for her. 'He might have done something wrong and be hiding somewhere,' she said. 'But I don't think he would have. Or perhaps he's lost a lot of money and doesn't want to tell Mum. But he makes quite a lot with his writing, so that doesn't sound right. He might', she added thoughtfully, 'be doing secret work – you know, MI5 or that sort of thing – and he isn't able to tell anyone about it, not even Mum. I think that's the most likely idea, and he's probably been sent abroad. What do *you* think, Flo?'

Flora, who was of a prosaic turn of mind, was fairly sure that Harriet's father was where he was said to be; in the churchyard with a great many flowers strewn above him. But she did not like to say so; it seemed cruel to dash Harriet's convictions. 'It's no use asking me,' she said. 'You're the one with the ideas, though some of them are a bit weird, I must say.'

Harriet sighed. 'I hope he comes back soon,' she said. 'Nothing's the same at home without him; I'm glad school's starting next week. Flo?'

'What?'

'D'you think your mother would let me stay tomorrow night as well?'

'I expect so; course you can. It's snowing,' Flora commented.

'How do you know?'

'I can see through this gap in the curtains.'

Harriet clambered across to Flora's bed and peered out. They watched the flakes fall softly, silently against the blackness of the night until, mesmerized by trying to count them, the two girls grew cold and dived under their duvets for comfort.

*   *   *

Two weeks later, Ellie went to London to meet Alex. She travelled by train, unaccustomedly daunted by the idea of driving and the hassle that would entail: the searching for meters, the traffic, the one-way systems, all of which she had grown unused to. Once the mechanics of the funeral were over, the emotional shock seemed to effect her more rather than less. Her moral and physical strength dwindled, and panic attacks hit her without warning, leaving her shaky. Coming out of one of these in a supermarket, feeling horribly infirm, she was frightened enough to seek help. The medication she was given made no noticeable difference, but she took it obediently, suspecting it was nothing more than a placebo. The house gradually emptied; Cass and Luke went back to university and school, and Harriet was only at home in the evenings. The worst moment of all from Ellie's point of view came as she watched her mother drive away down the lane and disappear from view, taking her wisdom and her unobtrusive support with her.

'I'll stay as long as you want me to,' she had told Ellie, 'but the longer I am here, the more difficult you are going to find it when I eventually leave.' She was embroidering a tapestry cushion cover, and did not look up from her work. 'It does get better in time,' she added, 'the pain; it has to, or one wouldn't survive.'

But how about the anger, Ellie wondered? Does that recede with time also? Close as she was to her mother Fleur, the circumstances of Philip's death were left unmentioned. Ellie's father had died young of a heart attack; a tragic but respectable death without any of the question marks that hung over the abrupt end to

40

Philip's life. The fact that she and Philip had been far from happy for that last year or so did nothing to alleviate her grief; on the contrary, she was unable to settle down to mourning him properly. A story lay behind their estrangement, and a reason for killing himself, for she knew instinctively that it was suicide. She guessed that other people suspected as much; people like Charles Stormont, Philip's erstwhile employer, who seemed to feel unduly responsible for the tragedy. But she realized that the subject would never be raised; it was a grey area into which, for kindness's sake, no-one would wish to stray. It hurt her deeply to think of the extremes of misery that Philip must have gone through alone, as if he did not trust her. However unpalatable the truth, whatever the demon that had driven him, to know was far preferable to groping blindly in the dark as she was now doing. She hoped – and feared a little – to come across some clue amongst his papers, but apart from finding the necessary legal documents and policies, she had not yet started to sort out his study. Going through his clothes and packing them for charity with her mother's help had taken all her emotional strength.

She gazed out of the window as the train swayed and rattled her towards Paddington, her mind on Alex; broad, solid, dependable Alex, brother of Philip and so very different. If he were jealous of Philip's fame and good looks, he had never shown it, but then he had his own quiet brand of charm. It occurred to her that he might have insight into a side of Philip that she, for all their years of marriage, had missed. Her spirits lifted very slightly at the thought of time spent in his company.

* * *

'You must try to eat a little; you can't afford to lose any more weight.' Alex ran his eyes down the menu in search of something to tempt her appetite.

He had harboured a secret love for Ellie from the moment Philip had introduced her into the Stavely family. He kept his feelings strictly under wraps, allowing them to show only in the small kindnesses and attentions he paid her. These would generally come in the form of presents; unusual rather than elaborate ones that might invite comment, and given as from himself and Cleo, although any accompanying card was always in his handwriting. He spent happy hours in junk and antique shops, looking for the bizarre or the frankly pretty to amuse her, or in second-hand bookshops for poetry and first editions. The nearest he came to declaring himself was to send her a Victorian valentine card, wonderfully preserved with all its bows and lace filigree paper intact. Ironically, the romantic gesture was lost: Ellie imagined that it came from Philip who was away filming, and described it to Alex in detail. Occasionally he wondered whether she had any idea of how he felt about her, and thought that most probably she did; women were intuitive, and Ellie rather more than most. In any case it made no difference; her whole world revolved around Philip, and he, Alex, had Cleo.

Sometimes he found it difficult to remember why he had married Cleo in the first place, or exactly when he had asked her. They had lived together for a while, grown used to each other and drifted into matrimony as if by mutual agreement, a year after Philip's and Ellie's wedding. He supposed the main purpose of the exercise had been to have children, but the children had not arrived, and it transpired they never would.

Cleo was really very good about it, throwing herself into charitable work as a substitute, and to use up her abundant energy and talent for organization. Privately, Alex thought these qualities would be better employed in running her own or someone else's business, but since they had more than enough to live on and there was no necessity for her to do so, he kept his ideas to himself. There was nothing to distinguish their relationship from many others; the excitement had long since been ironed out of it by familiarity, but they had learned to tolerate one another's habits and foibles. The result was contentment rather than unadulterated happiness. Alongside this mundane situation, love for Ellie burned steadily and discreetly without being a bother to anyone.

'How about the grilled scallops?' he suggested. 'Or a Dover sole?'

'Scallops would be lovely,' she answered. 'Please don't be cross if I can't finish them, though.'

Her thinness worried him; in two weeks of not seeing her, she seemed to have lost yet more weight. She had arrived at the flat in Ladbroke Grove wearing the same red coat, the vibrant colour accentuating the pallor of her skin. He had insisted on her having a drink and the alcohol had brought a flush to her cheeks, while he explained, as far as he could, the financial implications of Philip's death. It was his suggestion that they should get this discussion over and done with before lunch so they could relax. She listened almost in silence, very occasionally asking a question, her expression like that of an attentive but puzzled child finding herself in an alien environment. Alex, trying to concentrate on what he was saying, found himself wanting to bundle her into his arms, murmuring reassurances about her future. Ignoring the desire, he did his best to make plain what her assets amounted to. Philip, to Alex's surprise, had left his affairs in reasonably good order, and the life insurance alone would enable Ellie to keep the house if she wanted to. She would not be unduly rich, but she could live without worries if things were managed sensibly, whether or not she continued to work.

'Teaching English and drama to a class of little girls doesn't make much difference financially,' she told him, smiling for the first time. 'But I expect I shall go on doing it because I enjoy it.'

Their discussion over, they had walked round the corner to a small restaurant in Holland Park Avenue, where Alex had booked a corner table. While they waited for their order, they talked about Cass and Luke, and Harriet in particular; Ellie was worried that she had refused point-blank to accept Philip's death as fact. 'She seems to think that it's all an elaborate hoax, that he's gone missing and will eventually turn up again,' Ellie told Alex. She took a sip of white wine. 'You know what she's like, inventing things. I honestly don't know how to deal with the problem.'

Alex did not answer directly. He was taken up with surreptitiously studying Ellie's face, half turned to him with the high cheekbones and wide mouth, and the slight cast in one of her hazel eyes which he found so endearing. 'Would you like me to talk to her?' he offered. 'I may not be successful, but I can try.'

'Yes, please, if she goes on blocking it out of her mind. Children have more confidence in men; she might believe you.'

There was a pause while a waiter placed plates in front of them and topped up their wineglasses. Ellie ate a small mouthful, to show willing, so Alex guessed, rather than from hunger. 'Is it all right?' he asked.

'Delicious.' She looked at him. 'You know, it's wonderful to be here.'

His heart leaped with pleasure. 'I'm glad.'

She turned very faintly pink.

'It's not just that it's good to see you,' she said, 'although that goes without saying. You see, you're the only person I can talk to about Philip. People, even close friends, avoid the subject; terrified of upsetting me. I suppose it's understandable, but I long to tell them it makes everything worse, as if he never existed.'

'It always struck me', Alex said carefully, 'that you and he had a very special love. It was almost as though there were no need for other people in your lives. Friends were nice to have around, but there was no real necessity for them.'

'Did we really appear so self-absorbed?' she asked wonderingly.

'Dear Ellie, that's not what I meant.'

She stared unseeingly at the food in front of her, nudging it with her fork. 'Perhaps we were like that once,' she said. 'Things changed. Philip changed.'

'In what way?'

'He fell out of love with me.'

The simplicity of her statement stunned him; of all the explanations she might have given, this was the least expected. He cast his mind back to the last few times he had seen Philip; ever since he had started to spend part of the working week in London, they had met quite frequently for a drink or lunch. Alex remembered thinking that he looked rather tired, but then Philip had had the sort of ravaged looks that made women want to cosset him, even as a boy. Nothing about him had seemed otherwise unusual.

'I don't know what to say,' Alex confessed to Ellie. To ask her how she knew would be impossibly naive and intrusive.

'There's no need to say anything,' she replied. 'It happened. What I don't know, and you might be able to help me over, is *why*. He must have been having an affair, I'm sure of that; he was so obviously miserable, but he denied it.' Alex watched her long thin fingers fiddling with her wineglass. 'It probably isn't fair to ask you, but did he ever say anything to you about it, anything at all? He was very fond of you.'

'No, he didn't.' He covered her restless hand with one of his, full of pity at her expression. 'I doubt if he would have confided in me in any case; Philip kept matters very close to his chest. There was a lot of chat, and at the end of it one realized that one hadn't learned a thing. Could you', he asked, 'possibly be wrong about him?'

She shook her head. 'No, Alex.'

'No,' he echoed her. After a pause, he said gently, 'Forgive me for asking, but is it so very important to you to know the who and the why and the wherefore, now that it's in the past?'

She turned her head sharply to face him. 'That's just the point: it isn't in the past for me; it's right here with me the entire time.' Her voice, slightly raised, was almost impatient, as if he were being obtuse. Two women lunchers at the next table, sensing drama, temporarily stopped talking. Alex raised his eyebrows significantly.

'Sorry,' Ellie said quietly. 'I didn't mean to snap.'

'It doesn't matter. Is that all you're going to eat?'

She popped a last morsel of scallop into her mouth. 'I'm afraid so.'

'Coffee? Brandy?'

'Both, please.'

When the waiter had come and gone, Alex said, 'I'm not being much help, am I?'

'You're always a help,' she told him warmly.

'Perhaps if you explain rather more, I might understand.'

She paused, gathering her words. 'It isn't the fact of Philip having had someone else in tow that hurts me; it's his refusal to tell me. For the last two years he practised a sort of silent withdrawal – it was, frankly, hell – and nothing I did or said could break it.' She patted a bowl of brown sugar into shapes, unable apparently to keep her hands still. 'It wasn't the first time he'd been unfaithful; there had been two other brief flings, but they weren't important and he told me about them. I was furious at the time, but I got over it quite quickly. I always knew it was me he loved; I never doubted it for a moment, until he started to shut me out.' She glanced at Alex. 'That was what it was like, a kind of partition coming down between us.'

Alex said thoughtfully, 'And never a word of explanation. Are you certain it was a woman? It might have been problems at work.'

'There weren't any,' she said. 'He and Dominic had forged a great partnership as screenwriters; they had really taken off. Anyway, if that were the case, he would have shared it with me. We shared most things,' she added.

Alex watched her anxiously, wondering if she were about to cry, but she was dry-eyed. He suspected from her transparent look that she had wept herself out of tears.

'If you were to discover something about this – this unknown catalyst, how would it help you?' he asked.

'I'm not sure,' she said, 'but I would be that much nearer to understanding what happened to Philip. If I knew that, I might be able to put it behind me and remember him without anger.'

'Is that really how you feel?' he said in surprise.

She looked at him, and he saw that it was indeed true. 'Bitterly angry,' she said. 'Why not? He shut me out of his life and then left me. I can't stop thinking about how despairing he must have been to kill himself, and it was all so unnecessary. He would still be alive today if only he'd trusted me enough to explain, and that's the greatest blow of all.'

Shaken by her revelations, Alex stirred his coffee slowly and in momentary silence. He had had no idea of any rift between them, nor of Ellie's anguished convictions that apparently had been festering inside her. In the aftermath of Philip's accident she had touched once upon the possibility of it being suicide, but then the inquest had produced a verdict of accidental death and the subject had not been mentioned again. Secretly, Alex himself had doubts about the verdict, which he had admitted to no-one, least of all to Ellie; best for all concerned to allow Philip to rest in peace. But he was alarmed for her; he could easily imagine her brooding turning into a fixation, and wondered, doubtfully, whether she would agree to professional help. She broke into his thoughts before he could suggest it.

'I've shocked you,' she said. 'I expect there are rules about bereavement and the emotions attached to it.

48

Grief is all right and anger most definitely isn't.' She adjusted one of the combs that held her pale blonde hair in place. 'I shouldn't have told you; you were so close to Philip, and what I said was probably hurtful.'

He touched her shoulder and felt a strand of hair brush his fingers. 'I'm not hurt,' he answered, 'only worried for you. I don't want negative thinking to take over your life; it might be wise to have counselling—'

'No,' she interrupted with abrupt vigour.

'It works for a lot of people.'

'Not me, I'd clam up in front of a stranger. I don't really approve of rushing off to have your traumas sorted out by someone else, even if it *is* the trend.'

'Point taken,' Alex said mildly. 'It was merely an idea.'

'Oh, Alex! I'm sorry.' She rested her elbows on the table and put her head in her hands. 'I don't know what's got into me. I was longing for your advice and all I've done is to argue like a spoiled cow.'

'Stop saying "sorry",' Alex told her, quite forcefully for him, 'that is, if I'm to continue to offer my modest suggestions. It's the only annoying thing about you, this habit of apologizing.'

She smiled, a proper smile, the first he had seen for a long while. 'I thought you might discard me after today, I've been such a pain.'

'As an executor, I can't abandon you completely,' he replied with mock solemnity.

'Do you mind standing in as my counsellor?'

'I don't mind, Ellie, but don't expect me to be objective about it.'

Her forehead creased. 'I don't understand.'

'It means I'm too bound up emotionally with you – and with memories of Philip – to be dispassionate, and

49

therefore I'm not the best of advisors. Also, I shall try very hard to take your mind off the past so that you can start living again. Seriously,' he added.

It was snowing when they left the restaurant, flurries of small flakes blown by a spiteful north wind which settled briefly on Ellie's hair and Alex's balding crown. She unwound her long velvet scarf and draped it over her head like a peasant in a Bruegel painting. He offered to drive her to the station, but she was already hailing a taxi and lifting her face to his to say goodbye. Her lips were cold beneath his and he kissed her: a light sexless kiss befitting a brother-in-law.

'If you must keep looking back,' he said, 'try to remember the good times as well as the bad. I'll call you very soon.'

The taxi moved away to join the stream of traffic and he started to walk home, wondering as he did so whether she shared his sudden sense of desertion.

Chapter 3

It was the walled garden that had finally decided Ellie to make an offer for the house, satisfying, in so doing, a longing to own one that went back to childhood and the illustrations in books such as *Peter Rabbit* and *The Secret Garden*. The walls of the Old Rectory garden at Darlingford lived up to her dream of rose-red bricks weathered and softened by age, with narrow paths to match, intersecting what had once been a lawn but, by the time Ellie first saw it, had become a meadow. The house, facing south-west towards the distant downs, was as square and unassuming as a child's drawing, its Georgian frontage hiding from view the seventeenth century origins which splayed out in a jumble of rooms and outhouses at the back. Two white gates at each entrance to the semi-circular drive completed a pleasing picture of symmetrical tidiness that fascinated her. Try me, the house seemed to say, live here and no harm will come to you. Its orderliness was somewhat misleading; it turned out to need a lot doing to it. Half-heartedly, she looked at other properties, but it was only a gesture to keep Philip happy. He regarded the Old Rectory as a liability whereas she thought of it as a challenge, and it took all her powers of persuasion to smother his doubts.

'Dry rot,' he said when a floorboard crunched beneath his foot. 'And a leaking roof; you can see where the water's run down that wall. It's going to cost an arm and a leg to put the place right.'

'Just think how much we could knock off the asking price,' she pointed out coaxingly. 'A survey would be bound to be awful: we could make a ridiculous offer.'

They were standing by the wide sash window of what the agents had euphemistically described as the master bedroom. Philip lifted the two-year-old Cassandra onto his shoulders and held her firmly by chubby legs. Opposite them a hill rose gently; a path like a pale ribbon wound its way upwards and disappeared into a wood, feathery with the new green of spring.

'Great view,' he conceded.

Ellie rested her head on his shoulder, knowing she had won. 'We'll be able to grow peach trees on the south-facing wall,' she told him.

'That's what I love about you,' he said, kissing her hair, 'you can always be relied on to get your priorities right. Houses may fall to pieces, but at least the peaches will flourish.'

'Don't mock,' she said. 'A real English peach is a very serious matter. Come and see the room I've planned for your study.'

'Study! Actors don't have studies.'

'You will, from now on. Somewhere to shut yourself away from a growing family. You'll bless me for it one day.'

'Cass is no problem. Are you, Cass?' He pulled gently on each of her legs.

'You wait. There'll be two of them by the winter.'

Her second pregnancy was the reason for moving; there wouldn't be room for them all in the flat in London, and to be based in London was not the

52

necessity it had once been. Philip was established, as far as any actor could be said to be established, and more involved with screen than stage. He was away so frequently on location that it made no difference where Ellie was based; it was becoming increasingly impossible for her, with one-point-two children, to follow him wherever he went. The important factor was to make a home, and she found herself yearning for the country and her grass roots, but not without a degree of uncertainty about the possible isolation. It was her mother Fleur who tipped the scales in favour of Darlingford; it was she who discovered a photograph of the Old Rectory in a local estate agent's window, and sent the details to Ellie. Darlingford had the attraction, quite aside from the charms of the house, of being a mere 18 miles from Fleur's home; no distance at all in country terms. Both of them were happy about the proximity. Fleur, who was the least possessive of mortals and never demanded access to her granddaughter, nevertheless looked forward to seeing more of her; and Ellie foresaw, a little guiltily, the chance to dump the babies occasionally and join Philip while he was away.

She had tried hard to resign herself to the stretches of time that they were apart. After all, she had no illusions about stage relationships and the inevitable separations that went with them. They had both wanted children and she did not regret the decision for a moment. But she could not help looking back, every so often, to the early days when there had been no-one but themselves to consider, and life had centred round the success or failure of the next audition, for both of them. Nobody had coerced her into giving up her career to have a baby; Cassandra was well worth it, and in a way Ellie found it a relief, for she had known for some time that she would never be better than second rate. It was the sharing of a mutual occupation with Philip that she missed; the participation in the highs and lows, the excitement and the despondency, as if by dropping out she had severed a minute but crucial thread that helped bond them together.

They had met in a Midlands repertory company, playing the juvenile leads. Philip had already been there a month when Ellie arrived on a cold damp Saturday in October, fresh from drama school and riddled with nerves. Her digs, when at last she located them, did nothing to raise her morale; the landlady greeted her suspiciously, as if anticipating trouble, and in Ellie's small dark room there was a list of warnings about the plumbing system, mealtimes and noise pollution. The house smelled depressingly of stale shepherd's pie overlaid by disinfectant. Cheated of a longed-for bath by the lack of hot water, she had set out to find the theatre, so that she would know where to go the following day for the read-through of the next production. The doors were open for the evening performance; on impulse she bought the cheapest ticket possible and wandered round the foyer examining photographs of the cast. In a week's time hers would be amongst them, taking the place of a stunningly beautiful girl who had landed a part in the West End. Equally striking, in a dark haunted way, was the photo of her male counterpart. Feeling more intimidated every minute, Ellie had taken her seat in the back row of the stalls, and there, from the moment of Philip's entrance, she had fallen irretrievably in love.

The first week was taken up with rehearsals. Anna

Bailey, the girl whose photo had made Ellie despair about her own looks, was not present; she was in the last week of *Time and The Conways* before leaving the company on Sunday. But she was amongst them when most of the cast drifted to the pub, and it became obvious to Ellie that Anna and Philip were a pair. They sat together while he played with her long dark hair and teased her with the kind of in-jokes that were only possible between lovers. Ellie gritted her teeth, rehearsed furiously, and tried to accept the fact that where Philip was concerned she did not stand a chance. During rehearsals, when Anna wasn't around, he treated Ellie with untroubled warmth and friendliness which, in her state of mind, she construed as patronizing, and retaliated with a childish display of sarcasm. He remained irritatingly charming. It was not a propitious beginning, and for ten days she teetered on the edge of breaking her contract and leaving; almost any job seemed preferable to her present one.

On the first night of the new production, things began to improve, apart from an agonizing attack of stage fright. Philip came to her in the wings just before her entrance, took her shaking hands in his and kissed her on the cheek. She was too overcome by nerves to feel anything but gratitude for the gesture of sympathy.

'I'm going to be sick,' she groaned.

He squeezed her hands. 'You'll be brilliant, once you're on.'

In fact he was right. Brilliant was an exaggeration, but within the first five minutes she had the heady sensation of being in command. The experience was new to her, and it was so precious that she was terrified of losing it in subsequent performances. But the part suited her and her luck held for the whole of the fortnight's run. Her performance even drew a few words of praise from the producer, Jerry Carpenter, a man not known for scattering them lightly. With the boost to her confidence, she found the components of her life with the company slotting into place. The members of the cast were no longer strangers and she had been accepted into their warm, gossipy and occasionally acerbic coterie. Other people's relationships were of endless interest to them and, when Philip wasn't with them, they discussed Anna for the benefit of Ellie, who had scarcely known her. Michael Penfold and his partner Gerald Wright were particularly condemning.

'She was a bit of a bitch.'

'Had her claws into poor Philip before you could blink.'

'Such a waste,' Michael sighed. 'He really is to die for, don't you agree, Ellie?'

Ellie made a non-committal noise and buried her face in a mug of coffee.

'Don't be so partisan,' said Marsha Young who played the middle-aged parts. 'Whatever else, Anna is a beauty, contemporarily speaking. The face of the Seventies. She couldn't act, of course, but you can't have everything,' she added.

'Well, give me Ellie any day,' Michael said, patting her hand. 'Her face is far more interesting, it says something. And those eyes – I just adore the little irregularity in the left-hand one, darling.'

'Her legs are wonderful,' Gerald observed. 'Exactly like a boy's.'

'Shut up,' Ellie protested mildly. 'I feel like a prize heifer. Lord knows what you say behind my back.'

'Only nice things,' Michael assured her. 'We're fond

of you. I hope our Philip appreciates you,' he said, absently picking a blond hair off her jacket.

'We get on fine,' she said.

'I know, darling. That's not quite what I meant.'

She knew what he meant; they were all watching, without malice, to see whether she and Philip would carry friendship a stage further. Ellie did not dare let herself think about it often; she had had to work very hard to get her feelings under control in order not to give herself away. They were, she supposed, as close now as they could be without becoming lovers; it was inevitable, in their tight-knit little community, that they should get to know each other well. Fortnightly repertory left little enough leisure time, but what there was they generally spent together, either in wine or coffee bars, or in Philip's digs, which were more congenial than hers, hearing each other's lines and discussing everything under the sun. Families, friends, ambitions, books, music, all were mulled over – with the exception of Anna. She was first mentioned one wet Sunday afternoon when they had made instant coffee with Philip's electric kettle and were huddled in front of the gas fire, Ellie in the one armchair and he in a beanbag that he had bought in the town.

'I had a card from Anna yesterday,' he said out of the blue. 'The production is closing in two weeks' time. Bad luck for her.'

'Rotten,' Ellie agreed; and then, because that did not sound completely sincere, she said, 'With her looks, she should be snapped up for television.'

'Funny you should say that. She's about to go for an audition. They're casting for *Bleak House*.'

'Oh, good,' Ellie said, and they lapsed into an

unusual and not quite comfortable silence. She tried to glean from his profile what was going through his mind, but all she could see was the familiar outline and a flop of dark hair.

'Are you in love with her?' she asked, and immediately regretted it.

He twisted round to face her. 'With Anna?' he repeated, sounding genuinely surprised.

'Sorry, I just wondered. You don't have to tell me.'

'There's nothing to tell.' She watched the smile take over his face and transfer it in the way that made her heart double its speed. 'I'm fond of Anna,' he said. 'We had a lot of laughs, but she's not a girl to be taken seriously; not by me, anyway.'

'She's very pretty.'

'Very,' he agreed, 'and rather thick.'

'I thought men were supposed to be frightened of clever women,' she said.

'The really clever ones don't make it obvious.'

'The voice of experience speaking, is it?' she said mockingly, unable to prevent herself.

He ignored the remark as she had noticed he did quite often to avoid confrontation. Uncoiling long legs, he heaved himself upright and went to lean over her in the armchair. His face wore its sombre expression. Then he kissed her long and thoughtfully, withdrawing at last abruptly to say, 'Let's have some coffee. Shall we try that tricky scene in Act Two? I'm not happy with it.'

'Philip?'

'Mmm?'

'Where do we go from here? Am I to be just another Anna?'

'No, you're definitely not.' He looked down at her. 'If

58

you mean, is the next logical move to go to bed, the answer is yes. But not just yet.'

She fiddled with the frayed edge of her jersey. 'Because you're not certain, I suppose,' she said.

'No, because I do take you seriously and I want the moment to be right. There will be a moment.' He took her mug from her. 'By the way, there's a room here that's vacant. Why don't you leave that hell-hole and move in?'

She did not need any urging. Philip helped her transport her things and within a week she had exchanged her acidic landlady for the comfortably proportioned and easy-going Mrs Campbell. It was as well that Ellie moved when she did. Shortly before Christmas she caught flu and fainted dramatically on stage after the final Saturday-night curtain. The whole of Sunday she lay alternately burning and shivering under the bedclothes while Philip brought her hot drinks and forced cold remedies down her. In the best of theatrical traditions, she was on stage for Monday's performance, her legs feeling like strands of spaghetti and her voice threatening to give up at any second. They were a bad few days; her acting suffered, on one occasion she skipped a whole page of script, and Jerry Carpenter, who did not recognize illness, lost his temper. By the end of the week she was morally and physically drained. Philip found her late at night huddled in bed and weeping copiously, a box of tissues beside her. She was wearing a man's cardigan over her nightdress and her face was shiny from mopping. He sat down on the side of the bed and put his arms round her, and waited until she had finished her bout of crying, pressed against his chest. When she had snuffled to a halt, he carefully removed her cardigan, covered her up, undressed and climbed in beside her.

'It's no good,' she protested feebly. 'I only want to sleep.'

'I know,' he said. 'It doesn't matter.'

She gave a muffled snort of laughter. 'I thought we were waiting for the right moment.'

'And so we have. Wait and see.'

Eighteen months later, Philip had been given a leading role in an unpretentious, low-budget film which, contrary to expectations, won instant acclaim and more than one award. Suddenly, from the status of unknown actor, his name had become common knowledge and he was being compared to Olivier and Burton in their youth. Ellie was hardly surprised; she had privately expected something like this to happen sooner or later. She had not, however, been prepared for the publicity in which, as his girlfriend, she was inevitably involved. They were photographed everywhere together; coming out of restaurants, arriving at the airport after a holiday, walking in the street loaded with supermarket bags. Philip very seldom smiled for the cameras, although on the rare occasions that he did so it was with such startling sweetness that the picture usually appeared on the front page. Ellie grinned obligingly to make up for his sombre image, and wondered whether this was a passing phase of their lives or something that she would have to get used to, like royalty.

One of the pleasantest aspects of Philip's success was the increase in cash flow. After leaving the Midlands and coming to London, there had been a depressing gap when neither of them was working. Although the euphoria of living together was at its height, existing on very little money was still a strain. There were moments when they regretted putting repertory behind them, but Philip had been offered a part in a television thriller, and Ellie, despite the realization that her attitude was unprofessional, found she was too much in love to be left behind. They were lucky enough to be lent a flat in Fulham by Philip's brother Alex, who was being sent by his firm to their New York office for a year. 'We can't pay you much,' Philip told him. 'Peanuts, in fact, unless something miraculous happens.'

Alex had taken his eyes off Ellie with difficulty. 'Not to worry,' he said. 'At least you won't break the place up.'

Philip had been given a favourable write-up in the television review columns and Ellie made a detergent commercial, after which they had filled in with temporary jobs, waited for the telephone to ring and tried not to lose heart. He modelled for a mail-order firm and drove his clapped-out car as a minicab until it ceased to be roadworthy. She worked in a delicatessen and took dogs for walks in the park. They became adept at eating cheaply, and gave pasta parties for friends, who brought bottles of raw red wine and stayed late into the night, bemoaning their unemployment. Ellie minded this state of affairs more for Philip than for herself, not purely through altruism, but because he was passionate about his acting, whereas she did not have the same dedication. Much of her ambition had secretly dwindled since being with him, as if her love for him left no room for other emotions. Sometimes she frightened herself by such total absorption; she would wake in the night and peer in the semi-darkness at his face, the brooding ironed out of it by sleep, and wonder what on earth she would do if anything happened to him. She guessed he did not love her in the same all-consuming way, that whatever he felt for her was tempered by distraction, as if he were afraid to give away too much of himself. But she made him happy, and she meant more to him than anyone else in his life before. She knew this because he was constantly telling her, putting his arms round her at odd times, when she was cooking or pulling on her tights, and she believed him.

In the film that brought him success, he played a bisexual graduate torn by affection for a girl and love for a male friend. It entailed a love scene between the two men, the thought of which gave Philip sleepless nights beforehand. He reiterated his revulsion so forcefully that Ellie, sympathetic to begin with, grew impatient.

'It can't be *that* explicit,' she said. 'The censor wouldn't pass it.'

'It's OK for you,' he replied, pushing a hand through his hair. 'You haven't read the script. Rolling around naked in a wood with another guy doesn't leave much to the imagination.'

'It'll probably be a terribly quick shot,' she said consolingly. 'Over in a minute.'

They were sitting on Alex's pale-blue sofa, drinking whisky. It was meant to be in celebration of Philip having been given the role.

'How would you feel doing it with a woman?' he asked, refusing to be reassured.

'I wouldn't like it.' She giggled. 'I suppose I'd lie back and think of England – and the money, of course.'

'Well, I'm glad you think it's funny,' he said coldly, taking his empty glass to the kitchen and returning with it refilled, without offering to do the same for Ellie.

He slumped back in his place on the sofa. 'It's easy to be flippant when you're not facing the firing squad.'

'I'm sorry, darling.' She curled her legs under her and leaned against him, remembering his kindness to her when she had been shivering with panic in the wings of a Midlands theatre. 'I was trying to jolly you out of your gloom; I'll be serious from now on. I didn't realize you had a phobia about homosexuals.'

'I don't.' Mollified, he encircled her with his arm. 'I don't care what the hell they do together, as long as it doesn't involve me.'

'I do understand, but it was bound to happen to you eventually; that kind of scene, I mean,' she said.

'Meaning I look queer?'

'No, stupid.' She kissed him, 'but it's a topical issue; people are writing about it. You're professional; you'll manage, honestly.'

He had, of course, been exceptional, and his dark haunted looks were perfect for the part. When Ellie watched the scene which had caused him so much anxiety she felt a genuine wave of jealousy at its authenticity. The film was shot partly in London and partly at a magnificent eighteenth-century mansion in Devon, where she joined him once for a few days, staying at a pub in the nearby village. It was hardly worth the journey; Philip was tired from the long hours and slept for most of any spare time. But on a Sunday when there was no filming they went for a walk on Dartmoor, armed with sandwiches and a bottle of wine, and picnicked by a stream. The day was warm and larks sang high above them in an untrammelled sky of deep blue. They sat with their backs against a boulder in the shade of silver birches, drank from cardboard cups and listened to the splash and gurgle of running water slipping over stones. A kingfisher skimmed downstream, an exotic dart of colour, and was gone in a flash. 'Did you see that?' they asked each other in one breath, and laughed with pleasure. He stretched out on the short-cropped turf and put his head in her lap.

'You know what it means when you speak the same words at the same time?' he said.

'No. What?'

'It means you're perfectly in tune; your minds are working in tandem.' He peered upwards into her face, squinting against the sun. 'Would you say we're compatible?'

'Not always; not when you're being a shit,' she answered, twining a hunk of his hair in her fingers. 'Why do you ask?'

'Because I'd like us to be married.'

There had been a pause in which all the small sounds of the afternoon, the flowing stream, the birds, even their breathing seemed to increase in volume, while Ellie thought hard about her answer. Marriage had been one of those things she supposed they might get around to some time in the future. That she should suddenly be asked for an on-the-spot decision threw her into a state of confusion. She felt too young for babies and housekeeping and all the things that such a step entailed.

'It's a very grown-up thing to do,' she said slowly. 'I'd like to think about it for a bit.'

'If you have to think,' he said pessimistically, 'then you don't really want to.'

She plucked at a tuft of grass. 'It's not that,' she told

64

him. 'I'm actually rather frightened. Supposing it all goes wrong?'

'It won't. But anyway, it's the wrong attitude.' He sat up abruptly and kissed her, pressing her quite painfully against the boulder. 'I love you,' he said. 'How long is it going to take for you to make up your mind?'

She hesitated. 'A few weeks. Let's leave it until you finish filming.'

He sighed. 'You disappoint me. It's a wonderful day and a wonderful place for making an important decision.'

'Better on a rainy day when everyone's grumpy and nothing's going right,' she said with wisdom. 'It's less misleading.'

Until she became properly engaged the following autumn, Ellie had not met Philip's father. His mother Marge and her mother Fleur had both visited their offspring at the Fulham flat from time to time, bringing presents; smoked salmon, in Fleur's case, and a bottle of Gordon's gin from Marge. In fact, they had met each other there, and got on surprisingly well for two such disparate people. Marge had had a career in musical comedy from which Hugh Stavely had snatched her and committed her to a life of boredom and slavery – or so Philip, with grim humour, described his parents' relationship. Ellie did not know whether to believe him; she had very little experience of fathers and found Philip's antipathy towards his own unfathomable and rather sad. After they had broken the news of their engagement, they were summoned – again Philip's words – to spend a weekend with her future in-laws.

'Don't expect Pa to be nice to you,' he warned Ellie.

'It's nothing personal, just that he doesn't know the meaning of the word "charm".'

She travelled with an open mind, prepared to like everyone, and Philip with his face at its darkest and most haunted. The only thing that cheered him was the new Volkswagen with which he had replaced the old one and which he was now driving for the first time. The film had had its première and was already a box-office hit without a single bad review. His mother had been to see it and telephoned her congratulations.

'You are marvellous, darling! Well done, well done! I've hidden the review pages from Father; you know what he's like about what he calls poofters.'

'Thanks, Mum, but he won't be remotely interested in them,' Philip told her in resignation. His prediction turned out to be wrong.

The Stavelys lived in a Victorian Gothic monstrosity of a house smothered in virginia creeper and set in some of the loveliest countryside in Hampshire. Marge had put all her energies into the garden, where a lawn sloped down to a trout stream and a row of weeping willows. As they drew to a halt in the drive, she appeared at the open front door wearing a floppy straw hat and holding a trug basket, looking like a character from a Noel Coward play. A pack of barking dogs poured from the house and threw themselves at Ellie and Philip in good-humoured ebullience, ignoring Marge's feeble commands as she tried to embrace Ellie.

'Welcome, darlings! Shut up, hounds!' She shepherded them indoors. 'Guess what? Alex is here; he's brought a girl called Cleo. Lovely to have you *all*.'

'Oh good,' Philip said, who had spent some time persuading his brother into coming to lend moral support.

They had poured themselves drinks and sat around in the drawing room while Marge darted in and out to put the finishing touches to lunch. Alex quietly commandeered Ellie and told her about New York. He had recently returned, and she and Philip had moved to a rented flat in Chiswick. Ellie felt comfortable with Alex; tall, broad and bespectacled, he had nothing of Philip's photogenic looks, but he did have the ineffable quality of making one feel wanted. His girlfriend had what Ellie thought of as a neat face, with all the features the right distance from each other, and an air of confidence. She was dressed in a heather-coloured suit and glossy knee boots which made Ellie regret her own jeans and well-worn suede jacket and prepare to dislike Cleo, but she turned out to be so friendly and voluble that resentment was out of the question.

'Lunch is ready when you are,' Marge announced.

'Where's Pa?' Philip asked.

'Fishing. I don't think we'll wait for him.' She looked flustered. 'I think I should warn you; he's in a mood.'

'So what's new? What's set him off this time?'

Marge said apologetically, 'I'm afraid it's the film, darling. He thinks it's pornographic. So silly, I thought it was very sensitively done.'

'How on earth can he know if he hasn't seen it?'

'That's just the point.' Marge's large blue eyes were at their widest. 'He *has* seen it. He went up to London to his club, and after lunch he went to the cinema, and came home apoplectic. He takes more interest in you than you think,' she said, adding shrewdly, 'Take no notice, he'll soon calm down.'

Her advice was all very well, but Hugh Stavely was not the sort of man to be ignored, as Ellie discovered during the uneasy meal that followed. He arrived as they were all seating themselves at the dining-room table, and surveyed them from the doorway, a powerful figure in his fifties with greying hair and an aquiline nose that gave him a predatory look. He was introduced to Ellie and Cleo, whom he acknowledged crisply, and lowered himself with a thump into the carver at the head of the table. There was silence while Philip put a plateful of chicken and vegetables in front of him, and then everyone started talking at once. Hugh fixed Ellie, who was sitting next to him, with a stare.

'So you're the girl who's decided to marry Philip,' he remarked. 'We meet at last.'

Ellie, recognizing him for a man who would walk all over one if one let him, looked him clearly in the eye.

'We'd have visited before if Philip hadn't been working,' she said. 'I hope you're pleased for us.'

'That remains to be seen,' he answered obscurely, tackling his lunch.

'Of course he's pleased.' Marge raised her glass of wine. 'We all are. To Ellie and Philip, every happiness.'

'To Ellie and Philip,' they chorused.

'When is the wedding?' Cleo asked brightly.

'We haven't planned anything as yet,' Philip said. 'It depends on us both being free at the same time.'

'Are you working at the moment, darling?' Marge asked Ellie. She loved theatre talk.

'I've got a bit part in a television serial starting next week,' Ellie told her. 'It'll be a small wedding anyway; neither of us wants a grand one.'

'And how does your father feel about your marrying an itinerant actor?' Hugh demanded, making the description sound disreputable.

'Ellie's father died when she was small,' Philip

answered for her coldly. 'But if he were alive, I doubt if he would have been as bigoted as you.'

Hugh shrugged. Ellie felt her stomach muscles tighten in anger, and saw Alex watching her sympathetically across the table.

Hugh turned to Cleo. 'And how about you? You're not caught up in this stage business, are you?'

Cleo gave a little laugh. 'Heavens, no! My acting's so awful I never even had a part in the school play. I work for an interior decorating firm. Not nearly so interesting.'

Hugh grunted. 'A great deal more satisfactory, in my opinion,' he said.

'That's not what you thought when you first met me, Hughie,' Marge reminded him. 'You must have seen the show a hundred times.'

'I was young and foolish,' he said without looking at her. 'But I had the sense to remove you from it pretty rapidly.'

'And I *didn't* have the sense to refuse,' she said cheerfully. 'More peas, anyone?'

'Phil's been offered a contract with the RSC,' Alex said, taking the vegetable dish from his mother. 'There's something to be proud of, Pa.'

'What the hell's the RSC?'

'The Royal Shakespeare Company,' Alex told him patiently. 'Stratford-on-Avon.'

'Shakespeare, huh?' Hugh reached out an arm for the potatoes. 'Well, that can but be an improvement on the kind of drivel he's been connected with recently.'

'We saw your film,' Cleo told Philip with well-intentioned mistiming. 'It was terribly good.'

'On the contrary.' The serving spoon clattered back

into the bowl that Hugh was holding. 'It was merely terrible, nothing good about it.'

'Thank you, Pa, for those few kind words,' Philip said resignedly. 'Perhaps you'd like to tell me what you found disagreeable.'

Ellie watched Hugh's complexion turn a dull red, and held her breath. 'Just about everything,' he said. 'It was obscene. I don't mind telling you, I was ashamed to see a son of mine blatantly enacting a pervert. Bloody realistically, what's more.'

'Oh well, I'm glad my acting was up to scratch,' Philip said quite light-heartedly; but there was a white line round his mouth which Ellie knew meant temper.

'Come off it, Pa,' Alex said. 'It was a rather gentle portrayal of a love triangle. Homosexuality is a part of life; you can't ignore it.'

'I can, very easily,' Hugh retorted. 'Films like that shouldn't get past the censor; and you, Philip' – he glowered down the table – 'should have the sense not to get involved in any case. My God,' he added gloomily, 'I came away from that cinema wondering whether I really *had* spawned a poofter.'

'Now that's quite enough, Hugh,' Marge announced, her light soprano voice carrying an unusual ring of authority. 'Would anyone like more chicken? No? There you are,' she told him 'you've spoilt everyone's appetite, and I've made an upside-down pudding. Phil, will you help me clear?'

Ellie guessed her ploy was to remove Philip to the sanctuary of the kitchen and allow him to recover from his father's verbal onslaught. However, in the end they all found relief in carrying away the plates and dishes, leaving Hugh to glare moodily into space. For the rest of the meal he addressed his remarks to Alex and tried to persuade him to spend the afternoon fishing; but Alex, awkward at being so obviously singled out as the favourite son, refused, and joined the others for a long walk across the meadows. The evening was wonderfully relaxed; Hugh had gone to a Freemason's dinner, and they ate asparagus quiche on their knees in front of the television, and later got rather drunk and sang all the old music-hall songs from even before Marge's time. That night, Philip had failed to make love to Ellie, falling away from her in the narrow single bed with a groan of frustration. Marge had apologized for giving them separate rooms. 'So silly,' she said, 'but Hughie disapproves of cohabitation before marriage, as if he hadn't done enough of that himself. He's jealous, of course.' Lying beside Philip, feeling his body stiff with tension, Ellie wondered if jealousy really did account for Hugh Stavely's antagonism.

'He's such an angry man,' she murmured. 'It's as if he positively enjoys anger. Has he always been like that?'

'He's at his worst with me. Even as a child he disliked me.'

'Why?'

Philip linked his fingers with hers. 'I don't know. I suppose I didn't live up to his notion of the ideal son; tough, sports-loving, uncomplicated. Alex did better than me. I was a weedy little boy, a huge disappointment, and Mum was always defending me which only made things worse. The trouble is', he said, 'that I still mind about his disapproval.'

She squeezed his hand. 'You mustn't let him get to you.' She wanted to add: 'The distorted old fart isn't worth it,' but she sensed in him an innate grain of loyalty to his father despite their incompatibility.

'You've made a success of what you always wanted to do, and we've got each other. What he thinks doesn't really matter, does it?'

Philip sighed. 'I suppose not. But I'm terrified of growing to be like him, inheriting his intolerance and intimidating my own children. If I show signs of it, will you slap me down?'

'I'll do more than that, I'll divorce you.'

He turned on his side and pulled her close to him. 'We are going to have children, aren't we?' he asked.

'I expect so, some time,' she answered. 'Not just yet, though. I want you to myself for a bit.'

Eighteen months after this pronouncement of Ellie's, Cassandra was born. She had a shock of dark hair and thoughtful eyes which seemed to focus on Ellie, although she knew this to be impossible for a new-born baby. Philip was with the RSC, and most of her pregnancy had been spent in Stratford-on-Avon, where they had rented a cottage. She took a job in a bookshop; the pay was negligible but the work was peaceful, and wiled away the hours while Philip was at the theatre.

The idea of the baby worried her; its conception had not exactly been planned and she still felt emotionally ill-equipped to deal with the responsibility. Her love for Philip seemed so complete in itself that she was frightened there would be nothing left for a child. Her pregnancy had the opposite effect on him; he was fascinated, lying beside her in bed with a hand on the mound of her stomach to feel the baby kick, and buying up books on childcare. He fussed over her, insisting on doing the vacuuming, fetching and carrying and making her put her feet up, until she became mildly exasperated. 'It's *supposed* to be a natural process,' she protested, 'not an illness.' After Cassandra had shouldered her way into the world, Ellie decided there was nothing natural about it, and swore she would never go through such hell again. But a kind of peace descended on her as she watched the baby asleep in a cot beside her; she found her sense of inadequacy as a mother dwindling, and no longer had a secret wish to put Cassandra back where she came from. Accepting her for what she was, an extension of herself and Philip, it was as if Ellie had never been without her.

Chapter 4

Cassandra stood in a corner of the university car park, where she could keep an eye on Max Ehrhardt's Toyota, and waited for him to appear. His rooms looked out directly above her, and she huddled against the wall of the building in order not to be seen. She knew roughly when to expect him; he would be conducting his last tutorial of the day, which usually finished around six o'clock, give or take fifteen minutes. Her plan was to approach him as if by accident while he was unlocking his car, and cajole him into giving her a lift. With this purpose in mind, she had left her Mini behind that morning and travelled in by bus. She realized that as plans went it was pathetically obvious and he would see through it, but she was desperate to speak to him and could not think of an alternative way of going about it.

It had been a depressing term, following on the heels of her father's death while she had barely recovered from shock. The only thing that made the prospect of university bearable was the thought of seeing Max again. But she had returned after the Christmas holiday to find his attitude towards her had changed, and his manner was like that of any of the other tutors, friendly but impersonal. Gone were the warm meaningful glances and the pressure of his arm round her shoulders, drawing her closer. The clandestine dinners too had ceased, and the snatched glorious moments in a darkened car. There had never been many of these, but she had lived for them, and to have them withdrawn without explanation left her hurt and bewildered. She wanted to scream and shout at him to give her a reason for this sudden and dreadful remoteness, but somehow her frustration manifested itself in a sullen aura verging on the rude. Once, at the end of a tutorial which had gone particularly badly, her feelings had burst at the seams in an angry mutter.

'I don't see you alone any more.'

His eyebrows had risen; there was no softening of the eyes like there used to be. 'We're alone now,' he pointed out with maddening logic.

She shoved her textbooks into a battered briefcase with unsteady hands. 'You know what I mean,' she said furiously. 'Everything's different – you're different. Why?'

'Come off it, Cass. Circumstances change, pressure of work, and I do have a family, remember.' He had glanced at his watch. 'Listen, this isn't the time or the place for in-depth discussions. Another day, all right?'

And he had shepherded her into the corridor and hurried away with a wave of the hand.

That had been three weeks ago, three miserable weeks in which nothing was explained and her grasp of the Japanese language had not progressed one iota. She had isolated herself by her fixation; her peer group grew tired of trying to drag her out for a drink or a pizza. She generally refused, and in any case, she was no fun to be with. If it had not been for the fact that she had exchanged her lodgings for a rather scruffy furnished flat which she shared with her best friend,

Sarah Field, there would have been no-one in whom to confide. Sarah was aiming for a degree in psychology and was only too willing to practise on Cass.

'You've got a mega dose of the older man syndrome,' she said, sitting in their minute kitchen and biting into an apple. 'You're searching for a father figure to compensate for the loss of your own.' She eyed Cass speculatively. 'Understandable, but not advisable; they're always married.'

'You don't *choose* to fall in love,' Cass said bitterly, running her fingers through her dark fringe so that it stood up like a choirboy's quiff. 'You do talk crap sometimes, Frog. It has nothing to do with my father.'

Sarah said amiably, 'I didn't expect you to accept my diagnosis. Anger is a common reaction to the truth; that's a good sign.'

Cass looked at her friend's slightly protuberant eyes and wide mouth, which had given rise to her nickname, and thought how, if she hadn't been so fond of Sarah, she would have hit her.

As she waited for Max now, she remembered with bitterness her last tutorial with him two days before. His manner towards her had mellowed; perhaps he was regretting his impatience on the previous occasion, she could not tell. When their hour was up, he leaned back in his chair, turning a pen between his fingers, and surveyed her thoughtfully.

'It's not going well, is it?' he said quite gently.

She shook her head without answering.

'You've been through a bad time,' he went on, 'and I don't believe I've made allowances for that. I blame myself for being too tough on you. What you need is a break, try to relax, get out and do something different, preferably with a friend. I was wondering—'

He paused. Hope had surged through Cass in an unstoppable wave.

'I was wondering whether you'd like to come to supper at home,' he concluded. 'Jessica would enjoy meeting you, and we'll get the kids packed off to bed so that we have some peace. What do you think?'

She stared at him in disbelief at his insensitivity. How could he, how dare he blank out their moments together as if they had never happened, and relegate her to the role of student with problems? She wanted to tell him what to do with his family supper; words crowded her brain but somehow she could not utter them. In a voice she did not recognize she heard herself say, 'Thanks, but I'm pretty busy this week. Perhaps after the weekend—'

'Right you are,' he said cheerfully. 'We'll fix a day then. Take care.'

He was tidying papers on his desk as she left the room, his mind already on something else; she could see that quite clearly. She had let herself into her car and sat there for several minutes, trembling with mortification. Gradually her feelings hardened into resolution. In no way was she going to let herself be messed around; if he had grown tired of her, then he must be made to say so to her face. She had told Sarah as much on reaching home, slamming down her books and stamping about the flat restlessly. Sarah had observed that men like Max deserved castration, and he was highly likely to avoid confrontation if it were possible. In her view, she added, he wasn't worth bothering about.

In the car park Cass shoved her hands into the pockets of her leather jacket for warmth and shifted her weight from one foot to the other. A sharp east wind blew across the open spaces, bending the college daffodils before it. She had tried to rehearse what she was going to say to him without much success; she wanted to be dignified, not to sound like a child in a tantrum. She almost missed his emergence from the building; she was glancing at her watch, and when she looked up he had reached his car and had the key in the lock. He was not alone; a tall thin girl stood beside him, her straight blond hair blowing about her face. Cass knew her by sight but not by name; she was one of his first-year students, and judging by her carefree laughter at some remark he made, new to his attentions. He opened the passenger door for her, and there was a moment when Cass was tempted to run over to them, beat her fists on the car window and hurl invectives at him through the protective layer of glass. Nothing of the sort happened; instead, she watched them drive away until they were out of sight. When she finally moved, her legs were stiff from waiting, and the pain of rejection was sharp as the cold east wind.

Ellie propped her bike against the water butt by James Frobisher's back door and peered in at the kitchen window. The table was covered with a red gingham cloth, on which sat a coffee percolator, a jumbo-sized cup and saucer and an earthenware jug of narcissi. Of James there was no sign. At the back of the house half an acre of meadowland separated it from the seventeenth-century barn which served as James's workshop. The meadow was known as his wild garden and in another two months it would be filled with indigenous species of flowers, and alive with butterflies. Ellie passed through a wicket gate and followed

78

the narrow path that led to the barn, glad of her thick sweater and an anorak; it was late March and nearly Easter, but the air had not yet softened into spring. The barn doors were partially open and she could see James in blue overalls with his back to her, bent over a workbench. The smell of the workshop, a mixture of wood shavings, glue and beeswax, reached her before she stepped inside and spoke his name; tentatively, in case he was handling something delicate. At the sound of her voice he turned his head, then straightened to his considerable height and carefully placed whatever he was holding on the bench. 'Ellie, how are you?' He smiled, looking genuinely pleased to see her, his face creasing into folds like a bloodhound's.

'I'm all right, thanks, James.' And then, because she had known him a long time, she added, 'Why does one say that automatically even when one's feeling dreadful?'

'To stop people asking questions,' he said. 'Explanations can be tiring. How about some coffee?'

'You're busy.'

'Time I had a break.'

They walked back to the house in single file, James loping ahead to unlock the back door. In the kitchen he warmed up his breakfast coffee and poured it into bone-china mugs painted with roses. Almost everything he possessed, even the most mundane of household articles, had an attraction. Ellie had once remarked on the fact and he had replied that whereas a lot of people kept their treasures hidden away, he preferred to use them. His appreciation of beautiful objects might have gone hand in hand with a trying fastidiousness, but he treated possessions without any fuss or undue reverence.

79

He had bought the cottage and the barn that went with it twelve years ago, and had managed to maintain a certain anonymity. No-one in the village had discovered much about his past; it was common knowledge that he had been made redundant from a firm in the City and had built up a small but thriving business repairing antique furniture. The rest of his life, wives, girlfriends, relations, remained obscure, and what the inhabitants of Darlingford did not know they invented, so that when he first came to live there, rumours about him were rife. Since he turned out to be a helpful neighbour, and well liked, these gradually dwindled and he was accepted. He had the advantage of being an unattached male, and as such was much in demand socially, to be paired off at supper parties with lone women. Ellie admired his ability at these functions to be invariably friendly without divulging anything of himself from beginning to end of an evening. He had also become the man on whom people relied to help out, from dog and cat sitting to watching over their properties while they were away. It was with the intention of asking just such a favour that Ellie had called on him, slightly ashamed that she had hardly seen anything of him since Philip's funeral. She and Philip had befriended him before anyone else in the village had got around to doing so, but her unhappiness in the last three months had driven her underground, and James was not the kind of person to encroach on privacy. She leaned her elbows on the table and cradled the mug in her hands.

'I'm going to London for two nights,' she said. 'Would you mind very much feeding Mozart for me, and keeping an eye on the house? I'd ask Betsy Groves, but she's away taking care of her sick mother.'

'Of course. No problem. I'll sleep in if you think Mozart will be lonely.'

'Thank you, but he's not that sort of cat. He values his independence; sometimes I don't see him for days.'

'When are you going?'

'Tomorrow, until Friday.'

'I'll be there. Have you brought the keys?'

'No. I'll put them through the letterbox on my way to the station.' She smiled at him. 'You've very kind.'

'No problem,' he repeated. 'Doing anything interesting while you're away?'

She made a face. 'Meeting solicitors and bank managers. I never realized until now how a death in the family affects all aspects of life: things like wills, for instance.' She sighed. 'It's a necessity I could do without, but I'm lucky to have Alex to guide me.'

'Alex?'

'Philip's brother. You met him with us once, if you remember?'

'Slightly bald, glasses? I remember,' James said. 'Likeable, stalwart I should imagine.' He poured the remainder of the coffee into her mug. 'Divorce and bereavement are similar: each entails rebuilding a life, and that's not easy.'

She traced the pattern of the tablecloth with a finger, wondering whether his statement was an invitation for her to enquire further. 'You sound as if you know,' she said. 'Is that what you've done, built a new life?'

'I haven't finished,' he replied. 'I'm still building. But it's a dull story and I won't bore you with it.'

This, she felt, was a warning to stop probing. 'Well,' she said, 'I haven't even started; I don't know how or where to. Philip has left me with a mystery,' she added without quite meaning to, 'and I feel I can't get on with anything until I have an answer. Silly, isn't it?'

Tears pricked her eyes ominously, threatening to make a fool of her.

'Not silly,' he said calmly. 'There are bound to be question marks after such an accident.'

He rose, deliberately she guessed, to give her time to pull herself together, and carried the coffee percolator to the sink. 'I suppose you are quite certain you want an answer?' he asked with his back to her. 'There are times when the truth is more painful than living in doubt.'

'Not for me,' she said. 'Anything is preferable to unexplained tragedy.' She hesitated, but only for a split second. 'It's not just Philip's death I don't understand, it's the last bit of his life. Something went dreadfully wrong.'

He returned and sat himself down opposite her. 'I'm sorry,' he said. 'Really sorry.'

She stopped slouching over the table and sat up straight, giving him a brief smile. 'I'm being embarrassing; I didn't mean to unload my self-pity on to you. It's the lack of adult company that does it.'

He lifted his hands in an awkward little gesture of goodwill. 'I'm always around if you need to talk.'

'Thank you, James.' She reached for her anorak hanging on the back of a chair. 'I must be going; I've taken up enough of your time.'

'There's no hurry,' he said. 'I hope you discover what you need to know for peace of mind. Where will you start?'

'Letters,' she answered. 'That's all I have to go on.' She paused before saying, 'There's something else I'd like to ask; do *you* know what's happened to the public footpath and the stile where—?'

The question hung in the air uncompleted. He looked directly at her. 'The stile has gone and the footpath has been re-routed through part of the wood,' he told her. 'A hedge has been planted where the stile used to be. It seems a nice idea, encouraging wildlife.'

She nodded silently.

'There's nothing to see,' he said kindly. 'Absolutely nothing. But I imagine you won't want to walk that way in any case.'

'Not yet,' she replied. 'I dream about it, though. One day I might have to make myself, to chase away the demons.'

He saw her to the back door, ducking automatically to avoid the low entrance.

'You're not made for seventeenth-century cottages,' Ellie remarked.

'I had no choice. It came with the barn, and where else would I have found the perfect workshop?'

They stepped outside into sunlight forcing its way between thick layers of cloud. She retrieved her bicycle, feeling the unexpected warmth on her face, and thanked him once more.

'Take care,' he said as she started down the path towards the road. At the corner of the house she turned to wave. The overalls exaggerated his gangling figure, reminding her of a daddy-long-legs, and his untidy fair hair was lightened by the sun. She found the sight somehow reassuring.

Cleo had arranged a dinner party for the first evening of Ellie's visit. It was all part of her determination to 'take Ellie out of herself', so she told Alex, who listened with a sinking heart. Cleo got these zealous attacks

83

every so often and they generally led to some sort of trouble. A dinner party, he knew quite well, would be the last form of socializing Ellie wanted; he said as much to Cleo and was overruled. Selfishly, he disliked the thought of having to share Ellie with other people, but this he kept to himself.

She had been coming up and down to London regularly and soon their meetings would be rendered unnecessary by lack of business matters to discuss. This was her fourth trip and already he was having to think up valid excuses to see her. Probate was in the process of being finalized, a new will was ready for signing and the house had been reinsured. He had long since stopped pretending to himself that he was only carrying out his duties as a relative and executor, and settled for the fact that he had fallen in love with her; really in love, a subtly different feeling from the one he had had for her when Philip was alive. Marriage had put her beyond reach and it had never occurred to him to do more than fantasize about her. Unattached, she had become achingly available and very real, and his emotions, no longer restricted, were wandering all over the place. He did not know how to deal with them, and could not visualize himself doing anything positive. There was Cleo to be considered, and although he found her intensely irritating at times, he disliked the idea of hurting her. The situation upset his equilibrium and caused moments of the kind of light-headedness that he associated with youthful passions; so that when he met Ellie's train at Paddington and saw her blond head amongst the disembarking passengers, he moved forward on unsteady legs and with a thumping heart.

*   *   *

In Alex and Cleo's spare bedroom, Ellie unpacked the few things she had brought with her. She would have preferred not to be staying with them, but Cleo had suggested it too often for her to go on refusing. It was not through any fault of theirs that she would rather have been under her own roof: they were souls of kindness; quite simply, since Philip died, she felt safer at home. Safer from what or whom she could not say, and supposed the feeling sprang from anxiety, which in itself was a symptom of depression, according to the doctor. There did not seem much point in a clinical diagnosis or in the pills she had been prescribed and had recently flushed down the lavatory. In the end, she decided, she had to sort herself out; no-one could do it for her.

The flat gave her mild claustrophobia; Cleo was essentially an urban creature and had furnished her home accordingly. It was close-carpeted throughout in the same pale green; a sea on which footsteps made no sound. The noise of the traffic was muffled also by double-glazing, and Ellie, struggling with the bedroom window to let in some air, was faced with layers of glass that refused to move an inch. The central heating on the other hand was working overtime. Homesick for the draughts and the creaking boards of an old house, she went to the en suite bathroom, ran herself a bath and lay contemplating the immaculate décor and the glass bottles of salts and essences. Cleo's household ran on oiled wheels, literally; nothing for the comfort of the guest was forgotten. Ellie wondered whether this obsessive attention to detail had been born in her or was the outcome of having little else to do. She wondered as well if it got on Alex's nerves. They had scarcely altered over the years she had known them and it had always struck her as being a marriage without mood swings: stable and unexciting.

She dried herself slowly with the pink fluffy towel, her mind still on Alex. Much to her surprise she imagined going to bed with him. It was too late to feel ashamed; the thought had passed into her brain and lodged there before she could prevent it. She had never regarded him in this light before; he had always been Philip's older brother, caring, dependable, someone to lean on. Warm, comforting qualities, but not obviously seductive in themselves; and yet, now she thought about it, she was far from sure. She envisaged their relationship over the past weeks, slipping impercept- ibly from phase to phase of friendship, growing ever closer, and realized it would be easy to let it slide one stage further into love; not perhaps a grand passion on her part so much as an addiction to his protective nature. Since Philip's death she had felt no stirrings of sexuality; it was as if that part of her had died with him. It would be extremely awkward if it were to rekindle itself now, she told herself firmly, at the wrong moment and with the wrong person; a poor way to repay Cleo's many, if misplaced, kindnesses.

Full of resolutions, she dressed in a pair of silk trousers that Philip had given her at least ten years ago, added a cream silk shirt and caught her hair back in combs. Staring critically at her reflection in the mirror, it seemed to her that the hated cast in one eye was particularly pronounced, a symptom of tiredness or stress or, as in this case, of apprehension. Cleo was already in the drawing room, tweaking a flower into place in a talented arrangement. She was wearing a deceptively simple version of the little black dress and looked cool and composed and quite unlike the oven-flushed, garlic-smelling hostess with whom Ellie identified herself.

'There you are,' Cleo said. 'How lovely you look. What would you like to drink? I'm glad you're ready early; I've had an idea I'd like to discuss with you and there's time before people arrive.'

The train was crowded. Luke had a corridor seat; he did not know what to do with his legs. If he stretched them out they touched the ankles of the girl opposite; if he stuck them in the corridor they tripped people up. On the table in front of him the plastic mug of coffee and the plastic-wrapped sandwich sat untouched. The luggage racks were already full when he boarded the train and he had had to leave his suitcase and backpack by the door in danger of being nicked. He had left a lot of his gear at school, things like tennis racquets and games clothes, which you weren't meant to do because the premises were let during the holidays to overseas students. His mother usually drove over to collect him at the end of term; but this wasn't the end, it was two weeks early and his journey was unscheduled. He had been 'sent down', or 'rusticated' as they called it, and she knew nothing about it. He had tried to telephone her, but the answerphone was switched on. His punishment might have been worse; he had been caught smoking cannabis with two others in the fives courts, and officially the penalty for drugs was expulsion. All the same, he wasn't looking forward to explaining to her.

The three of them weren't particular friends, but they were all in the A-level form, and Paul Lyttleton and Luke shared a study. Paul was an owl-like academic boy whose parents had split up round about

87

the time that Philip had died, and their housemaster had placed the two boys together for moral support. Mark Conway, blond, florid and streetwise, had provided the cannabis, and they had smoked on and off throughout the term with impunity, until now. The headmaster, who ran his school on liberal lines, was keen to find a psychological explanation for Luke's sudden fall from grace.

'You know the rules. Can you give me any reason why you should not be expelled?' he asked in the calm tone that never varied.

Luke, facing him across the expanse of mahogany desk, hesitated, aware that the severity of his punishment depended on his answer. The truth was boredom and a desire to experiment, which would guarantee the sack. Impossible to plead that he had outgrown school with its regimentation and its smell of damp towels, foot-fug and boiled cabbage. Life, thank God, had more to offer and he had been impatient to grab it.

'I would like at least some kind of explanation from you,' the headmaster had prompted him.

'Yes, sir. Well, I've been really worried about what I'm going to do when I leave.' He wrinkled his forehead convincingly. 'I've decided I don't want to make music my career after all, and I keep putting off telling my mother; she'll be disappointed. It's been weighing on my mind. She's had a lot of problems, you see.'

This confession, while sounding cloyingly pathetic, had the merit of being both accurate and acceptable. Whether or not it had driven Luke to try dope was debatable. He had waited, the palms of his hands damp from nerves, not daring to hope for leniency.

'You have no excuse for bottling things up,' replied the headmaster. 'You are surrounded here by people ready to listen and advise, including myself. Anything else you're holding back?'

'I don't think so, sir.' Only nagging doubts that couldn't be mentioned, Luke thought, like the fear of girls who seemed to be born with a superior knowledge of the world. There were enough of them at school, for it was coed: a whole contingent of bright-eyed, bright-haired girls with aggressive breasts and knowing laughter, and a confidence he couldn't match.

'So, am I to understand that you resorted to drugs owing to a certain confusion about your future?' the headmaster had said without sarcasm.

It had sounded ridiculous put like that. Luke had had a sudden urge to say no, that wasn't how it was at all; he had tried pot because it was a new experience, had liked the mild euphoria it induced, and it was reputedly less harmful than alcohol.

'That's right, sir,' he said, giving the safe answer. 'Only cannabis, nothing hard,' he added unwisely.

'An illegal substance, nevertheless; the nature of it makes no difference, it's the principle that concerns me. By rights I should hand you over to the police, but since this is the first time any of you have been in serious trouble, I'm trusting you all not to reoffend. Once you start seeking addictive props every time you are faced with a problem, your future will be bleak indeed.' The headmaster leaned forward to deliver his standard lecture for miscreants. 'And another matter; you are privileged to be here, and with privilege comes duty. Those of you in the A-level form have a duty to set an example, which in this instance you have failed to do.'

Luke croaked an apology, cleared his throat and repeated it.

'I'm not going to expel you,' the headmaster said, and his words were sweeter than honey to Luke, who had not realized, up until that moment, how much he minded. 'For one reason alone: this term has been a difficult one for you following the death of your father and I'm taking that into consideration. I don't believe it will serve any good purpose to ruin the end of your school career. I shall rusticate you, all of you; you can go home tomorrow. And when you return for the summer, I shall expect an unblemished record from you for those final weeks. I'll be writing to your mother.'

'Thank you very much, sir.'

'When you get back, Luke, come and see me, and we'll try to sort out your future.'

'All that fuss over a couple of joints,' Paul remarked later. 'Bet you they'll legalize pot in a year or two.'

He and Luke were back in their box of a study. Relief at the outcome had restored their appetites and they were eating round after round of toast and marmalade.

'I don't believe Mike hasn't tried it himself,' Luke said irreverently of his headmaster. 'He's a Sixties guy; everyone was into drugs in the Sixties.'

'Our parents, probably.'

'Probably,' Luke agreed. 'It doesn't mean they're going to understand about us, though, does it?'

His cool attitude towards the trouble he was in was all very well in front of Paul. When alone and facing up to presenting his mother with a double disappointment, he felt very small and ashamed. In the immediate aftermath of Philip's death, while raw misery had made them tactile and uninhibited with each other, they had reverted to their original bond of mother and child, but it had not lasted. At school, he had deliberately tried not to think of her unhappiness; he told himself there was nothing much he could do about it, while in reality he was obsessed with his own sense of loss and how to deal with it. She wrote, stoical chatty letters; he replied by telephone, occasionally. He wished now he had made the effort to write back, guessing that this would have been worth a dozen phone calls to her.

The train had come to an inexplicable halt in a railway cutting. Primroses, already in bloom, were clustered across the steep banks. The girl sitting opposite Luke raised her head to look, chewing the end of her pen. He was vaguely aware that she had spent the journey writing on a pad of foolscap, making notes from a large volume lying open on the table. Her long brown hair hung each side of her face in curtains and she wore glasses, not the trendy kind but ordinary dull National Health ones. Luke idly summed her up as mousy and unfrightening. He unscrewed the lid of his mug of coffee, took a mouthful of the grey liquid, which was now lukewarm, and lowered it in disgust as the train started with a sudden precipitous jerk. Coffee slurped against the plastic rim, spattering the girl's writing with a rash of tiny stains. They stared at one another in silence.

'Oh shit! I'm sorry.' Luke searched his pockets for a handkerchief but she was already dabbing at the paper with a tissue.

'Wasn't your fault, was it?' she said, giving him a smile. 'I've got to copy them out anyway. It's only a rough draft.'

'It looks important.'

'It is.' She pushed her glasses on top of her head and rubbed her eyes. They were the best part of her, blue with dark irises. She reminded Luke of someone, but he could not think who. 'The end-of-term exams are in a week and if you don't pass, they can throw you out,' she told him.

'Are you at university?'

'Medical school, first year.'

He was impressed. 'Do you go round the wards in a white coat, that sort of thing?'

'Sometimes, not often. There's not much practical for the first two years; it's all theory, lectures. There's so much work,' she groaned. 'I know I'm never going to make it.'

'You must be clever or they wouldn't have accepted you,' he pointed out. 'Not like me, having to resit maths A level.'

'A lot of it is luck, passing exams,' she said, unwrapping a piece of chewing gum and offering him the packet. 'Getting given a question on something you read up the night before is about as likely as winning the lottery. So you're still at school then?'

'For another bloody term, yes.'

The middle-aged couple sitting in the window seats raised their eyebrows at each other significantly.

'I'll thank you to mind your language,' the man said, turning a disapproving face to Luke.

He jerked his head at the woman and the two of them pushed past and disappeared in the direction of the buffet car. Luke caught the girl's eye and they started to laugh.

'You certainly know how to clear a space round you,' she said.

'Simple,' he agreed, grinning.

'I suppose it's a nosy question, but shouldn't you be at school right now?' she asked.

'Shouldn't *you*?' he retorted, nettled.

'Yes. My gran's ill, and I've been over to Sherborne to see her.' She watched him, her head on one side. 'You're skiving, aren't you?'

'I'm not, as a matter of fact. They've kicked me out, sent me home.'

'Expelled you?'

'Only for the rest of the term; they're letting me back into prison for the summer.'

'Wow! What have you done?'

He sighed. 'You really are nosy, aren't you?'

'Yes, always have been,' she said. 'Go on, might as well tell me.'

'Oh, all right,' he answered, and gave her the story in three sentences.

'I've never done drugs,' she said. 'I'm too scared of getting hooked. Dealers used to hang around the gates of my old school, trying to catch kids of ten and eleven. Anyway,' she tucked the curtains of hair behind her ears, 'I don't have that sort of money.'

'Neither do I,' he said. 'I'm skint.'

'Will you cop it from your dad when you get home?'

'I don't have a father.' It occurred to Luke that he was saying the words for the first time.

'The same as me,' she said. 'At least, I have, but no-one's seen him since I was born.'

'I'm sorry.' He could not think of anything else to say.

'I don't mind. You don't really miss what you've never had.' She gazed out of the window at fields dotted with sheep and lambs, her profile untroubled. 'Spring in the country's great, isn't it? Wish I was going home like you instead of that grotty hall of residence in London.'

'Where d'you live when it's not London?'

'Near here. You know Stourton, the next stop but one?'

'That's where I'm getting off.'

'You are? Well, Mum lives at Darlingford, about ten miles away.'

'That's amazing!' he said. 'I've lived there all my life.'

'I don't believe it! Whereabouts in the village?'

'Near the bridge on the Stourton road; the Old Rectory.'

She leaned forward to peer at him more closely. 'I know who you are,' she said. 'You're Luke Stavely, aren't you? My mum works for your mum. I'm Hilary Groves. We used to play together when we were little, remember?'

'Not really,' he admitted. 'Perhaps I was too young. How old are you?'

'Twenty.'

'I'm eighteen. I expect my sister Cass would remember.'

'That's right: Cass.'

'I knew you reminded me of someone,' he said. 'You're like your mother; you've got the same colour eyes.'

They looked at each other and broke into laughter.

'It's really weird, meeting on a train, isn't it?' he said.

'Destiny,' she agreed with mock solemnity.

'I wonder why we haven't seen each other around since we were two or four or whatever?'

'I spent most holidays with Gran,' she told him, 'over at Sherborne, so Mum could go out to work. And term-times, I was at Stourton Grammar and you were at boarding school, weren't you? Funny, that, sending

94

your kids away to school, like kind of getting rid of them,' she said.

'I was sent there because it's a musical school and that's what I wanted to do,' he said. 'I got in on a scholarship.'

'And *you* said you were dim,' she reminded him.

'It was a music scholarship; I'm not academic.'

'Why run yourself down? A scholarship's a scholarship.' She looked at him with renewed interest. 'What instrument d'you play?'

'Piano and violin.'

'I can't play anything,' she said. 'I'd give a lot to be able to sit down at a piano and let it all flow.'

'It doesn't always flow. There are days when you just can't seem to get it right.' Out of the recesses of his memory there came a sudden vivid picture of his father, sitting at their upright piano and beating out non-stop jazz, switching effortlessly from melody to melody. 'Pa was a natural,' he said. 'He played by ear.'

'I remember *him*, too,' she said. 'He used to give us all those little bags of Maltesers; in your garden where we were playing. And Mum and I watched him on telly as Heathcliff in *Wuthering Heights*.' Awkwardly, without looking at him, she added, 'Mum told me about what happened; the accident, I mean. It must be dreadful for you. I'm really sorry.'

'Yes, thanks. It was a bad knock.' He liked this girl; she was the kind of person he could have confided in, but there wasn't time, and anyway, he had only just met her. He wanted to tell her that the accident theory didn't convince him or, so he suspected, his mother, but that the alternative explanation for Philip's death was too agonizing to be admitted. Instead, he fished an

95

old shopping list out of his jeans pocket and pushed it over to her, blank side up.

'I'll be coming to London soon,' he said. 'We might meet and go for a drink if you'd like. Where can I call you?'

'Great. Why not?' She jotted down a number. 'The phones are communal and forever engaged, so you have to go on trying.'

He looked at his watch. 'I'd better go and see if my gear is where I left it.'

She went with him and leaned out of the window to say goodbye as he stood with his luggage on Stourton station. She was wearing a shapeless baggy sweater that somehow accentuated her extreme thinness, and he found her lack of style endearing.

'Best of luck with the exams,' he called to her as the train carried her away from him.

'See you,' she called back, her straight brown hair blowing in the wind.

Alone again, he felt his isolation more acutely than before their chance encounter. He wished he had her companionship on the bus ride from Stourton to Darlingford, to cushion the mounting apprehension of facing his mother. It wasn't her anger he dreaded; her tolerance as far as her children were concerned was very nearly inexhaustible. But however well she appeared to accept the drugs incident and his second thoughts about music, she would not be able to hide her anxiety. The strain would show; he knew exactly how the expression in her eyes would reflect it, shading them as though a light had been put out. To make things worse, he was turning up without warning.

The burglar alarm was set when he let himself into

the house, and the windows were locked wherever he wandered. He had not thought of Ellie being away, had imagined her out for the day locally. There was a bowl of primroses on the kitchen table with a note in small neat handwriting propped against it. 'So many of these in the garden, thought you might like a few,' it read. 'Hope they last until Friday. All well here. James.' Luke replaced the note, feeling the anticlimax of her absence, wishing very much he did not have to wait to confess. He wondered where she had gone; there weren't many people she would choose to stay with at the moment, and Alex and Cleo were the most likely. Deciding he would telephone them later, in the evening, he fetched his luggage from where he had dumped it in the hall and lugged it to his bedroom. A bluebottle buzzed against the closed window, seeking escape. The room looked out over the front of the house to a distant view of the downs; and closer to home the chalk farm track snaked up a gentle incline towards the wood where Philip's life had come to an abrupt end. Luke turned away and threw himself on his bed with his eyes shut, overcome by the events of the past two days. In a fit of desolation, he wept for his father, the tears leaking from beneath his lids and running silently down his face.

The weekend after returning from London, Ellie continued her search for hoarded letters of Philip's. The study had been exhausted and yielded nothing, and she turned her attention to the attic, to rootle amongst its dust-covered contents like a pig hunting for truffles. The sound of children's voices reached her through the open window; Flora had come to spend two days with Harriet, and Luke was supposed to be keeping an eye on them while he mended a puncture on the wheel of his bicycle. He was also in charge of the baked potatoes for lunch. Despite her outward calm, Ellie was angry with him. Her initial reaction to his being sent home in disgrace was one of panic; drugs were beyond her, and she did not know how to handle the situation. After a sleepless night, the panic subsided and she began to get the facts into proportion, but a feeling of inadequacy persisted, making her short-tempered. The whole sorry incident, she persuaded herself, would not have happened if Philip had been alive. Or would it? Out of all three children, Philip had paid the least attention to Luke. She resisted the impulse to telephone Alex and ask for his advice, realizing that she was becoming unwisely reliant upon him for moral support. Only half her mind was on the job of sorting through a cardboard box full of correspondence; the other half had strayed to Cleo's proposition on the evening of the dinner party, which had thrown her into a state of uncertainty. Settled on the sofa with her pre-dinner drink, Ellie had taken the photographs which Cleo handed her, and listened obediently.

'The villa belongs to friends of friends,' Cleo explained. 'It's on Corfu, and they let it for the summer months. We've more or less decided to take it for three weeks at the end of July and thought what fun it would be if you all came as well. It sleeps eight people. What do you think?' She sat down opposite Ellie, slightly flushed from the brilliance of her suggestion, and waited, a little obviously, for a rapturous acceptance.

'I—' Ellie said, and stopped, groping for non-committal phrases. 'It's a lovely idea,' she went on slowly. 'Will you give me a day or two to think about it? There are things to be taken into account, money for one, and what Cass and Luke want to do. They've reached the age where they're apt to make their own holiday arrangements,' she added apologetically.

A look of disappointment flickered across Cleo's face, to be quickly gathered under control. 'I would have thought', she said, crossing her legs neatly, 'that *this* year they might want to be with you, all things considered.'

Alex had come into the room at that moment, freshly bathed and shaved, and poured himself a drink from an array of bottles.

'You mustn't bully Ellie into something she doesn't want to do, Cleo,' he said.

'She's not,' Ellie told him hurriedly. 'It's a terribly kind suggestion, and in theory I'd love to come. It's just that . . .' She hesitated.

'You'd like time to decide,' Alex finished the sentence for her.

'Well, time in which to ask the children,' she said. She peered at the photographs of the villa one by one, taken at various angles; a long, low white house surrounded by a terrace and oleander bushes. 'It looks marvellous,' she added enthusiastically, while part of her hunted for excuses as to why she could not possibly go, 'and rather expensive.'

'In fact, it's very reasonable.' He came to sit beside her, squeezing her shoulder in passing. 'In any case, that's my problem.'

'I'd want to pay my share.'

'Listen,' he told her. 'The whole point is for you to have a holiday without worries. If I couldn't manage it, I wouldn't have suggested it.'

'But the airfares,' she said feebly. 'Four of them.'

'I'd like to take care of those as well, but if it makes you feel better, we could go half-shares.'

'Alex, I can't possibly let you,' she protested.

'It would give me a lot of pleasure,' he said simply. 'If there's something else you'd rather do, then that's another matter, but you should get away for a while – with Harriet, whatever happens.'

'Thank you,' she said. 'Is it all right if I think about it and let you know next week?'

The doorbell had rung, and Cleo had left the room to welcome the first of her guests, saying over her shoulder, 'Do say yes; Alex and I get bored with each other on holiday.'

From then on Ellie had found herself in the midst of introductions, and the company of people who kept asking her how she was managing, briefed about her bereavement by Cleo, judging by their sepulchral tones. It was not until later, lying in bed sleepless after too much to eat and drink, that the uneasiness at Alex's offer crept back to her. Summer holidays reminded her acutely of Philip at the zenith of their happiness together; she could not imagine one without him. Neither was she able to picture herself as an alleviator of marital boredom between Cleo and Alex. Cleo's words filled her with misgiving; she had begun to see, with awful clarity, the plight of the single, middle-aged woman, reliant on other people's kindnesses proffered under sufferance, or when she could be of use. The fact that Alex was probably on the verge of falling in love with her made the situation worse rather than better; it would be only too easy for her to allow it to happen. Visualizing a holiday fraught with awkward moments, she was strongly inclined to wriggle out of it. However, there were the children to be considered; she put

100

the plan to Luke and Harriet when she returned home and they voted in favour of it unanimously, rather to her surprise and for varying reasons.

'I think it's a great idea,' Luke had said promptly, obviously pleased at any piece of good news to lift the shadow of his disgrace.

'Is it like Tuscany?' Harriet asked, Tuscany being her one experience of foreign travel.

'Not really,' Ellie answered. 'It's a Greek island, and the house is by the sea.'

'*Very* near the sea?'

'Right beside it.' She showed Harriet the photograph which Cleo had given her. 'You can walk to it down this little path. See?'

'Ooh!' Harriet breathed a sigh of sheer ecstasy. 'Can I go down it on my own?'

Cass did not display the same enthusiasm when Ellie telephoned her. She sounded flat and slightly impatient, as if her mother was interrupting whatever she was doing.

'I suppose we'd better go,' she said in answer to Ellie's question. 'Anything to get away from this dump after my finals in the summer.'

'You sound terribly disillusioned,' Ellie remarked. 'Are things going badly for you?'

'Oh, you know, no more than usual.'

No, Ellie thought, I don't know. What is it this time: man trouble, work, money? Cass's life at twenty-one had become a carefully guarded secret.

'I thought you might have made other plans,' she said.

'Chance would be a fine thing,' Cass said bitterly.

Ellie's patience broke, 'Something's wrong,' she snapped, 'that's obvious. If you won't tell me, then there's nothing I can do to help. But I very much hope you're not going to sulk all the way through a holiday organized partially for your benefit.'

Cass mumbled words down the line that Ellie did not catch. 'I can't hear you.'

'I said, I'm sorry.' There was a pause. 'Look, Mum, I've got to go. I'm in the middle of exams and there's all this revision. Tell Alex and Cleo I'd like to come on holiday, please.'

She said goodbye and rang off without asking Ellie how she was. Kneeling amongst the cardboard boxes and the battered suitcases in the attic, it occurred to Ellie that there were times when she did not like her eldest daughter. She loved her, but that was a different matter. It was impossible to say how much of Cass's prickly attitude stemmed from the loss of Philip. From an early age she had been closest to him, choosing him as confidant; and yet, Ellie now remembered, there had been a cooling off in her behaviour towards him in the months before his death, and the joking between them had more or less stopped. Ellie sighed; putting the problem of Cass from her mind for the moment, she went back to sorting letters, bewildered at the amount of junk that had accumulated over the years.

Harriet and Flora had invented a tracking game. Beyond the walled garden there was an orchard, and beyond that a paddock, which had once, before they had ever come to the house, been home to a pony. There was a stable in the corner, little more than a shed sheltered by thick hedges that ran round all four sides of the field. They took turns to be the 'goodie' or the 'badie'; the idea being for the 'goodie', who was given a head start, to reach the shed and rescue an imaginary hostage without being seen; crawling along the deep ditches by the hedges until she reached the cover of some conveniently placed conker trees. The 'badie' was at liberty to follow, but she risked choosing the wrong side of the field and missing her quarry. The alternative was for her to sit amongst the branches of an apple tree in the orchard and simply keep her eyes skimmed. Flora favoured the latter method. She preferred being the 'badie'; she was altogether too solidly built to make a successful quarry, whereas Harriet seemed to vanish like a wraith.

Hostages were much in the forefront of Harriet's mind; they provided an explanation of her father's disappearance, yet another in a succession of ideas. The hostage she imagined in the shed was Philip, chained up and languishing in a dark dank cell. He had been missing for eighty days; she had marked off each one in the green leather five-year diary which Granny Fleur had given her for Christmas. Every time she had a new inspiration about his whereabouts, she wrote it down. Whenever she felt angry with him, which was only occasionally, she would read back the excuses she had made for him, to remind herself that his absence wasn't his fault. She did not tell her mother any of this; in fact she had stopped talking about Philip altogether, knowing that it upset Ellie. It made Harriet feel very alone; she was the only one in the family who refused to believe in Philip's death. Luke had talked to her about it, and Harriet knew it was because Ellie had asked him to: 'try to make her see reason,' she would have said. She loved Luke, but what he had said had made no difference.

'Pa's dead,' he had told her bluntly. 'He had an accident and he died. People do. You're refusing to

103

admit it to yourself because it hurts, but you'll have to eventually.'

'Why will I?'

'Because I'm telling you the truth. He had his funeral and I was there.'

'I wasn't, though,' she had said. 'You didn't *see* him dead, did you?' she added accusingly.

'No, but other people did.'

'Who?'

'Alex.'

'Why?'

'Because', Luke said patiently, 'he had to identify Pa. Someone had to; it's the law.'

Harriet's eyes widened. 'That's horrible! It couldn't have been Pa; he's gone away somewhere.'

'Oh, come *on*, Harry,' Luke said wearily. 'Of course it was Pa. Alex is his brother.'

Harriet covered her eyes with her hands and buried her head in a cushion. 'Stop it!' she said in a muffled voice. 'I shan't listen!'

Later she had cried from sheer frustration. It took a lot of determination to go on believing in something when everyone told you you were wrong. Crawling on hands and knees now, she reached the end of the ditch and wriggled forward to the protection of the nearest tree. Flora hadn't shouted 'seen'; Harriet suspected her of not even bothering. The shed, when she looked in, was empty as always of everything except a hay rack built into one corner. She felt suddenly bored with the game and dispirited; Luke's voice yelling 'lunch' came as a welcome interruption.

Ellie sat on the floor of the study, four postcards and an incomplete letter spread out in front of her. Philip's old and worn briefcase, which she had brought down from the attic, lay beside her. After a fruitless search for the right key, she had had to force the lock with a screwdriver. It struck her as odd that he had bothered either to lock it or to put it upstairs amongst the junk. Even now, with the evidence of what she supposed was an affair laid out before her, she wondered at the necessity of hiding it so carefully. The small bundle of correspondence, bound with an elastic band, had been laid on top of a pile of photostatted scripts; the cards enigmatic in the extreme, the letter rather more explanatory, and all of it unsigned. She read them through once more, as though by doing so she might discover some clue to Philip's death that she had missed: 'Sleepless in LA, midnight. Wish you were here. Call you soon,' *'Je ne regrette rien.* Et tu?', 'A stupid misunderstanding. Hated leaving on a sour note. Please forgive', 'Things progressing well. Will fax you about date of return'.

There were no postcodes on the cards, pointing to the fact that they had arrived in envelopes, and they all depicted views of Los Angeles and its environs. The letter had no heading.

'Darling P,

I suppose it was too much to hope you'd understand that my feelings for you are unchanged and will remain so. No-one can take away the love we had, and still have, for each other. But whereas you have a separate and complete life with your family, I have nothing. It is this futureless prospect that I cannot face any longer. We went over and over this ground last night into the small hours and I don't want to rake it up again. They were the worst hours I have ever experienced, and the despair in your face when I left was the worst aspect of all. *Try* to see that this isn't a farewell; I am merely putting myself on the same footing as yourself. Is that so hard to accept? Please, if you care, give me some kind of reassurance.'

That was where it ended, at the bottom of one side of a sheet of writing paper; any continuation apparently lost or deliberately destroyed. Slowly Ellie gathered up all that was strewn on the floor, put it back in the briefcase and rose stiffly to her feet. She walked to the French windows and stared out at the garden. The daffodils were past their best and clumps of white and yellow tulips were coming into full bloom. The evenings, she noted in a detached way, were drawing out. There was no joy in the coming of this spring; the portents of it had to be shared to be of any significance. Bleak anger, directed at the faceless woman who had taken Philip away from her, invaded Ellie, and she shivered in the dampness of the late afternoon. Despite her suspicions, confirmation of his adultery had come as a shock; she realized that she had not seriously expected to find evidence of any kind. Now that she had done so, she was no nearer understanding the despair to which he had apparently been driven. She had opened one door only to be faced with another, and without much hope of discovering what lay behind it. Alex was right; she should have left the whys and wherefores of Philip's death alone; knowing them would not bring him back. And yet to know had become an obsession, and obsessions were not that easily squashed.

Luke opened the door and put his head round. 'The

girls are hungry. Shall I fill them up with that chocolate cake in the larder?' He advanced into the room without waiting for an answer. 'Is something the matter? You look spooked, Mum.'

'I've been going through Pa's papers,' she said, forcing a smile.

'Oh, I see, yeah. Shall I make some tea?' he asked awkwardly.

'No, thanks, I'll do it. I need a break. I'll be with you in a moment.'

She pushed the briefcase into the knee-hold space of the desk, turned out the lamp and followed him towards the cheerful noise of *Neighbours* on television.

Chapter 5

The middle years were the best, the ones that Ellie liked to recall, when the children were at their most endearing, and Philip's career was at its height. Those years were pinpointed in her memory by dozens of small incidents linked haphazardly to form a panorama of their lives; celebrations and minor disasters intermingled. After each of his successes they made another improvement to the house; a loft conversion followed the television production of *Wuthering Heights*, the addition of a new bathroom followed the big screen version of *Henry V*, and so on. There was no lack of work; it seemed that he was in demand for almost every prestigious production that was being cast for cinema or television. Hardly a week went by without his dark intense looks appearing in the pages of some newspaper or other. On special occasions such as premières, Ellie would be by his side, her thick fall of blond hair groomed into artful shining submission. They were interviewed at home for a three-page article in one of the Sunday supplements, the camera roving lovingly over the interior of the house and garden, catching Cass and Luke lolling against their parents' knees and gazing into the lens with wide-eyed self-consciousness. 'Philip Stavely relaxing at home with his wife Ellie and their two children.' Occasionally Ellie was alluded to by the press as Fenella Carrington, the actress, although it was years since she had set foot on a stage or film set. She did not regret the fact; life was full enough as it was, trying to juggle her loyalties between the children and Philip. A large proportion of her time was devoted to propping up his belief in himself. He had always been a perfectionist; now self-doubt had crept in, increasing with every major role he undertook. Ignoring brilliant reviews and universal acclaim, he was never satisfied with his performance. He hated watching himself on screen; when it could not be avoided, after film rushes or a première, there followed the groans and the self-recriminations.

'Christ! I screwed up that scene,' he would cry, marching up and down the kitchen, or thrashing about in bed like someone in pain. 'I've lost the touch; can't act to save my life.'

'I see,' Ellie would answer with the calm born of long practise. 'So, the critics are wrong to a man, and you, of course, are right.'

She used to find these scenes wearing, but had gradually become resigned. Sometimes, not often, when she was tired or expecting her period, she would snap him up. Mostly, she allowed them to burn themselves out, like Luke's tantrums.

'Am I totally impossible to live with?' he asked once, holding her close in the dark silence of their bedroom.

'Not always,' she replied. 'I'll tell you before you drive me into leaving you. I just wish', she added, 'you didn't have to tear yourself to shreds; for your sake.'

He buried his face in her neck. 'I love you; whatever happens, don't ever forget that.'

'Why should anything *happen*?' she said, faintly alarmed.

'No reason. It's an expression, that's all.'

The days preceding a new production brought a different kind of nervous tension. He would shut himself in his study with the script and remain there, apart from meals, until he had familiarized himself with his next role. The study was strictly out of bounds at such times to all except Ellie bearing mugs of coffee. She allowed him three days of this hermit existence before she barged in on him and flushed him out into the light of day, inventing things for him to do like taking Cass and Luke for a walk, as if he were another child. There followed a period of time when he wanted to discuss with Ellie every nuance of the character he was to play, shamelessly interrupting whatever she was doing. Cass, who from eight onwards knew each step of this routine of her father's, and was inordinately proud of him, waited for her turn, when he would learn a few lines especially for her to hear. She would sit on an upright chair in the study, her feet dangling and her eyes solemn beneath her dark fringe, a stubby forefinger pointing the way down the page of script. Luke, excluded from this ritual on account of his extreme youth, would express his chagrin in howls of rage, and had to be placated by Ellie with chocolate biscuits.

There were the long stretches of time when Philip was in work, and the house would seem peaceful but strangely flat without him. Ellie felt relief at the sudden lack of pressure for a day or so, followed by a sense of depletion, and she would immediately start making plans to join him wherever he was working. She could never be away for long because of the children, but even a few days were better than none. The dangers of lengthy separations were obvious, particularly so in a

110

profession where simulated passion was apt to become reality. Ellie was privately jealous of all his screen lovers; but she had discovered that to meet them face to face over a drink in the pub, when they were tired and their hair needed washing after a day's shooting, alleviated her feelings for them enormously. Her mother Fleur would stand in for her in her absence, happy to have her grandchildren to herself. But it was Betsy Groves who did the shopping and cooked for them all, and who knew whom to contact if one of the children were ill. Ellie did not know how she would have managed without Betsy.

She had entered their lives by coincidence rather than design; a tall, angular woman with black hair twisted into a knot at the nape of her neck and a tanned skin as if she worked out of doors. Ellie, newly arrived in Darlingford, had seen her in the village riding an old-fashioned bicycle, with a small child strapped in the seat behind her, and wondered about her. It was January before they met, on a raw wet morning guaranteed to dampen the most ebullient of spirits. Ellie was exhausted. She had discovered the hard way that to move house just before Christmas with a new-born baby and a toddler was foolish in the extreme. Philip was in London for a television series, her mother, who had helped her over the holiday, had returned home, and the Old Rectory seemed daunt-ingly large after the flat. To make matters worse, Luke was a miserable baby who cried by day as well as night. Ellie, used to Cass who had been comparatively easy, was driven frantic with anxiety and lack of sleep, sympathizing in her worst moments with infant mur-derers. On this particular morning she put the baby in the pram after his feed, dressed herself and Cass in mackintoshes and gumboots, and set out to walk to the village shop. Sometimes, if she were lucky, Luke would fall asleep to the rhythm of the pram.

The shop sold most things and had recently become self-service. Ellie took a wire basket from a stack of them, balanced it on the pram and went along picking items off the shelves as rapidly as possible; Luke's golden silences did not last long. Cass wandered in her wake clutching a bottle of fabric softener, which would have to be put back where it came from. The shopping completed, Ellie stood in the queue for the post office to buy stamps, rocking the pram with one hand while holding on to Cass's warm paw with the other. The dark woman with the bicycle stood in front of her, her own child controlled by leading reins as she collected what looked like a benefit pay-out. Luke stirred, sneezed and began to grizzle. Ellie decided to forget the stamps and pay for her groceries before his grizzling developed into yells. Another queue built up behind her at the counter while her shopping was put into plastic bags, mostly pensioners full of good advice as Luke worked himself into a fury. 'Colic,' one remarked confidently. 'My Jack had it something terrible.'

'Teething, most like,' another said sagely.

'It could be the milk. Feeding him yourself, are you, dear?' someone asked.

Ellie fumbled in her wallet for a note and answered grimly in the affirmative. Luke was now sounding like a car alarm. She stuffed plastic bags onto the rack beneath the pram, hoisted Cass into the toddler's seat and left the queue to argue amongst themselves about child rearing. In the street the rain slashed in her face vindictively as she trudged home and let herself in at the back door. Luke's squawls continued relentlessly while she divested Cass of her dripping mac and sou'wester and threw them with her own over a kitchen chair.

'Why don't he stop?' Cass asked disapprovingly.

'Good question.' Ellie began unpacking the shopping. 'We'll change him, shall we?'

It was then that she discovered that the disposable nappies were missing, left behind in her rush to leave the shop. She thought of the two remaining ones in a drawer upstairs and the second trip she would have to make, and knew total frustration.

'Damn and shit!' she said explosively.

'Damn and shit!' Cass repeated with accuracy.

The doorbell rang before she had time to explain the wrongness of swearing. On opening the back door she found the dark woman, all but unrecognizable in a black hooded cape, holding out a carrier bag.

'You left this behind in the shop,' she said, balancing her bicycle with her free arm while rain dripped from the edges of her hood.

Ellie felt a rush of gratitude. 'Oh, how kind you are! Have you come miles out of your way?'

'No, I live just over the bridge, in one of the cottages there.'

'Well, anyway I can't thank you enough,' Ellie said above Luke's bawling. 'Why don't you come in?' she added doubtfully. 'I'll make some coffee if you can stand the noise.'

'I'd like that,' the woman replied, rather to Ellie's surprise, and unstrapping her child from its seat, walked past Ellie to the kitchen as if she knew the way. 'Better hang the coats, else they'll wet your floor.'

113

'There's a row of hooks by the back door,' Ellie said, filling the kettle.

'Hang yours, too, shall I?' the woman said, and scooped them up without waiting for an answer, her small daughter trailing her like a shadow.

'My name's Ellie – Ellie Stavely,' Ellie said, spooning instant coffee into mugs.

'Yes, I know. They told me in the shop. I'm Betsy Groves and this is Hilary.'

'Would you mind making your own coffee, Betsy?' Ellie asked, looking wildly at the pram. 'I'll have to see if Luke's wet.'

'Is it OK with you if I pick him up?' Betsy asked.

Ellie pushed a weary hand through her hair. 'I wish you would,' she sighed. 'Quite frankly I'd like to get him adopted.'

'That bad, is it?' Betsy lifted the purple-faced baby and laid him against her shoulder, steadying his head with one hand. He gave two or three piercing yells and stopped abruptly; there was a blessed silence broken only by a few exhausted hiccoughs.

'You're a miracle-worker,' Ellie breathed. 'He never stops for me. What do you do that I don't?'

'Nothing, except you're probably all tensed up and I'm not. They sense that; it's different with other people's babies. Like me to change his nappy while I'm about it?'

Ellie opened the packet and handed one to her. 'I didn't mean to use you as a nanny,' she said apologetically.

'No problem. I like babies,' was Betsy's reply.

When Luke had been put back in the pram to sleep without a protest, Ellie supplied the two older children with milk and biscuits and made the coffee.

114

'You've certainly earned this,' she said as she handed Betsy a mug. 'There's a permanent job here if you ever want one,' she added jokingly.

Betsy's eyes roved round the kitchen as she sipped her coffee. She had a face like a wood carving, with high cheekbones and a firm jaw, and she looked as if nothing much would surprise or unsettle her.

'Looks like you could do with an extra pair of hands,' she remarked. 'It's a big house, isn't it?'

'Just at the moment it seems enormous,' Ellie said, conscious of the unwashed breakfast things in the sink and Cass's toys scattered about the room.

The two little girls had finished their biscuits and were staring at each other suspiciously.

'Why don't you build a castle with Hilary?' Ellie suggested to Cass hopefully, pushing forward a trolley full of plastic bricks. After due thought, Cass squatted on the floor, chose an orange one and held it out to Hilary with reluctance.

'I'm afraid she's not very used to other children,' Ellie confessed.

'Nor Hil.' Betsy finished her coffee and went to rinse the mug. 'Still, you've got another one coming on. Luke'll be company for her in a while.'

'Is Hilary your only one?'

Betsy turned. 'Yes, and likely to go on being,' she said flatly. 'We're a single-parent family. Is this all right to dry my hands on?'

Ellie nodded and decided to pry no further. 'Perhaps we should start our own playgroup with Hilary and Cass as founder members,' she said brightly.

'That's a thought.' Betsy rolled down the sleeves of her black sweater. 'Did you mean what you said about there being a job going here?' she asked.

Ellie said in surprise, 'I certainly meant it; I really need some help. But I had no idea you'd be interested.'

'I'm looking for work and I'm used to cleaning and children. I'd have to bring Hilary, though; the nearest nursery is Stourton.'

Ellie experienced a wonderful sense of relief. Already she could hear the sound of Betsy's key in the lock and her voice calling a greeting, and realized that not only was she overtired but also lonely. Someone to lean on, and to moan to. 'Bring whoever you want, the dog, the cat as well as Hilary,' she said, laughing, 'just so long as you come.'

Betsy smiled. 'How many hours do you want me for?' she asked.

'How about three? When can you start?'

'Say Monday around nine o'clock?'

'Great.'

Betsy had left soon after that, turning at the door with Hilary in her arms. 'You haven't asked me for a reference,' she pointed out with some severity.

'I don't honestly think I need to,' Ellie said.

'You should do; I'll bring one on Monday. How d'you know I'm not going to steal the silver?'

But Ellie had known, and time was to prove her instincts right. It was not until she and Betsy had become friends that she learned that Betsy's husband was in prison for armed robbery; and even so, she doubted her decision would have been different.

By the early summer of the first year Ellie and Philip were becoming an integral part of the social life of the village. Philip's fame had gone before him, and at first there was a certain amount of mistrust over his profession, particularly amongst the older residents.

Anything to do with the theatre was suspect; they regarded it in the same light as they did pop groups and envisaged wild and licentious weekend parties. When nothing like that happened, and the limit of Philip's entertainment of his house guests was a drink in the bar of the Bugler's Arms before lunch on a Sunday, their fears subsided and they accepted him as a serious actor without really knowing what was meant by that. The younger members of the community, who privately longed to get to know him and Ellie, held back from issuing invitations for fear of being seen as celebrity hunters. There were one or two mothers of small children with whom Ellie was on going-to-tea terms, but for some time that was where entertainment seemed to begin and end. It was Charles Stormont who eventually broke through these ridiculous social barriers; having no such inhibitions of his own, he merely thought Ellie a remarkably attractive girl and admired Philip's talents, and proceeded to do something about it.

Charles had been in his late fifties in those days; a diplomat who had taken early retirement and gone to live in Darlingford to write thrillers and manage the considerable amount of land he had inherited. He had settled in the pretty eighteenth-century manor which had belonged to his late wife's family and was known by the locals as the Big House. All this information was transmitted to Ellie by Betsy; he was, according to her, generally approved of, not least because he supplied a lot of people with work on the estate.

'A proper charmer,' she said. 'You should go and see the garden, you being interested. It's open to the public over May bank holiday.'

Ellie had gone on her own, leaving Philip to battle in

his study with a new script while Betsy babysat. The house was at the opposite end of the village, behind a high wall with wrought-iron gates and down an avenue of limes. She parked in the stable yard set aside for visitors' cars and spent an hour exploring; wandering through the woodland wild-flower walk, round the lake and into dozens of separate gardens hedged by immaculate yew. There was a nursery garden to one side of the grounds where she selected some plants and carried them on a wooden tray to pay. Charles Stormont was behind the till, wearing a baggy green jersey with a spotted dark-blue scarf tucked in the neck. Despite the lived-in clothes, he looked, so Ellie thought, entirely right for a diplomat, with a thin humorous face and a full head of hair brindled with grey. She dumped the tray on the counter, feeling awkward; there was the question of whether or not she was supposed to recognize him. So far he had waved to her from a car on the main street and she had waved back, and that was the limit of their acquaintanceship. He settled the matter by smiling and holding out his hand.

'Mrs Stavely? I'm Charles Stormont. You've put me to shame.'

'Oh, why?' She returned the smile. 'I'm Ellie by the way.'

'I've been meaning to get in touch with you since January and it's already May.' She looked puzzled. 'To ask you both to a welcome-to-the-village drink,' he explained.

'It doesn't matter,' she said. 'I've been fairly busy getting the house straight.'

'My only excuse is pressure of work. I've been trying to finish another book and keep to the deadline.' A small queue of visitors had built up behind Ellie,

118

clutching plants. 'Don't go away,' he said. 'I'll just attend to my job for a moment.'

She stood to one side until he had finished and turned back to her.

'Now,' he said. 'Let me rectify my lapse in hospitality and arrange for you to come round. How about next Saturday? Is Philip at home or working?'

'He's at home,' she said, 'between jobs. Saturday would be lovely.' Silently she hoped Philip would agree to be dragged away from his script. 'You have a wonderful garden,' she commented.

'You must see it when there aren't so many people around,' he said. 'I'll give you a guided tour when the roses are out. I'll put your plants in carrier bags. Double delphiniums and lupins; a good choice.'

He had refused to let her pay. 'A housewarming present,' he said, and getting a helper to take charge of the till, he insisted on carrying the bags for her to her car. 'I'm a great fan of your husband's,' he told her, and went on to ask intelligent questions about Philip's career, and to talk about his books.

'I'm always meaning to start on my memoirs,' he said. 'A light-hearted account, I hope; not one of those tomes that give one mental indigestion. I have a feeling I shall need help in sorting out the material; a kind of literary PA.'

'It sounds an interesting job for someone,' Ellie remarked.

He opened the car door for her. 'I suppose you wouldn't consider it?' he asked.

She laughed. 'I'd love to, but with two small children, I'm not the right candidate, I'm afraid.'

'Just a thought,' he said. 'Look forward to seeing you next weekend, about six-thirty.'

She had driven home with the satisfying knowledge of being found attractive. Charles Stormont might be old enough to be her father, but there was no mistaking the light in his eyes when he looked at her. He had also thought her intelligent enough to be offered a serious job. It made her realize how bogged down she had become with domesticity, and how long it was since she had felt like a woman in her own right. Her life revolved round two children under four and making sure nothing disturbed Philip's absorption with his work. She loved them all, and at the same time longed for change and a chance to flex her thinking processes, even if it were temporary. She tried to give Philip an account of her morning over lunch, but although he put on a show of interest, she could tell half his mind was elsewhere. The fact depressed her for the rest of the day, and she was unusually silent after Cass and Luke had been put to bed and she and Philip were having a drink. He eyed her speculatively over the rim of his glass. His sensitivity was not confined to self; it was one of the things she loved most about him, his immediate reaction to her moods.

'You're low.'

She thought of denying it and discarded the idea. 'Yes,' she agreed.

He crossed from his chair to her corner of the sofa and sat with an arm round her shoulders. 'Don't tell me, let me guess. You love me, and Cass, and Luke, but you're sick of the relentless routine of the daily grind. And then this morning you find a distinguished middle-aged man who flirts with you – quite rightly – and offers you an interesting job. You drive home in a nice warm glow of satisfaction, only to find yourself back in the same old rut with an introverted husband

120

stuck into another bloody script and the limited conversation of tiny tots. Am I right?'

She turned her head sharply to look at him, astonished. 'I didn't think you listened to a word I was saying,' she said.

'That's where you're wrong. And I *am* right, aren't I?'

'I suppose, sort of.' She smiled at him. 'Charles Stormont didn't flirt, though, and I never said he did.' She sighed. 'It's only a mood; it'll pass.'

He pulled her close to him. 'What you need is a break. We haven't been away since Luke was born. I shall sweep you off somewhere for a shamelessly hedonistic long weekend.'

'Lovely,' she said, 'but it won't solve the long-term problem.'

'Which is?'

'I want to work at something more demanding than domesticity before my brain becomes completely fossilized.'

'Are you regretting giving up on acting?' he asked.

'No. I wasn't ever going to be brilliant, and I should be terrified to start again now.' She reached for her drink and took a thoughtful sip. 'I think I'd like to teach drama, but I'm not qualified. Perhaps a school would accept me; teaching children might be fun. Anyway,' she said, 'it will have to wait until Cass and Luke are older.'

'We could employ a nanny,' he suggested a little uncertainly, 'if you think it's a good plan.'

She stared at him in horror. 'I can't think of anything I want less. They cost the earth, insist on using the car and I wouldn't have a moment's peace about her reliability.'

121

'Darling!' He sounded mildly exasperated.

She leaned over and gave him a quick kiss on the cheek. 'I know,' she said. 'I'm being impossible. Don't worry, I'll snap out of it now. Are we really getting a long weekend?'

'Of course. Where shall it be? Paris, Rome, Venice?'

'Venice,' she replied promptly.

A fortnight later they were installed in an unbelievably expensive hotel, while outside the rain came down like steel rods. It continued for the whole of the next day, and they spent the hours in bed, between real linen sheets embroidered with the initial C, listening to the sounds of traffic on the canal below until the evening. They made up for their decadence in the time they had left by exploring as far as possible on foot in the sudden heat of the sun; at night taking a gondola and seeking out restaurants for plates of seafood tagliatelli and wild mushroom risotto and bottles of dry white wine. Every evening Ellie would telephone home to her mother, unable quite to believe in the well-being of her children. The profligate four days had had the desired effect of jolting her out of her rut and giving her a fresh perspective on family life, at least for the moment.

Drinks with Charles Stormont the previous weekend had turned out to be a small party given for the purpose of introducing Philip and Ellie to a few of the local residents. It was the first warm evening of early summer and they had gathered on the stone-flagged terrace outside the open windows of the drawing room. She need not have worried about Philip's attitude; he charmed his way around his fellow guests meticulously. Watching him gaze into the eyes of a stout woman as if she were the one person present who mattered to him, Ellie smiled to herself in pride that he belonged to her; and then, because who knew how many fascinating women had received the same irresistible treatment, she had an old familiar twinge of anxiety. Towards the end of the evening, when most people had said their goodbyes and drifted away, Philip was left deep in conversation with Charles, and Ellie with a man whose wife was absent, and whose eyes kept slipping from her face to the cleavage of her black silk sweater. 'You must come to supper,' he said. 'Miranda would love to meet you.' Like hell she would, Ellie thought, and excusing herself, went to join Philip and slip an arm through his. Charles and he were discussing the merits of a play recently opened in the West End, and she sensed an instant rapport between them. Shadows had spread across the breadth of velvety lawn by the time they left with Ellie driving; Charles poured generous drinks and Philip was not strictly sober.

'He's an extraordinarily nice guy,' he said expansively. 'We must get him round; I'd like to see more of him.'

'I told you, didn't I?' Ellie replied.

'He asked me if I wrote,' Philip added, 'which is odd, because I've had this idea for a play going round in my head for some time.'

'You never said.'

'There didn't seem much point; it's only an idea.'

'Why', asked Ellie, circumnavigating their gateway with caution, 'don't you get it down on paper?'

'I might do that if there's a long gap between jobs.' He laughed. 'I've also been asked to open the village fête; apparently it takes place in Charles's garden in

June. I've never opened a fête before. What on earth does one say?'

'Something short, witty and to the point. Don't let the glory go to your head,' Ellie said drily.

Seeds for the future had been sown that evening, although neither of them knew it at the time. Not least, it was the beginning of a long friendship with Charles Stormont, from whom all the other issues stemmed. For Ellie, it remained for years just another genial summer gathering amongst many, and without significance.

When Luke was seven, he ran away from home; not far in terms of miles, although it seemed like it to him, but to the opposite end of the village. Facing the entrance to the Big House, there was a path that led first to a crooked black and white cottage, and eventually to a barn at the far side of a field. Fired by a sense of adventure, he walked until he arrived at the open doors of the barn, from which came the noise of hammering; and that was how he discovered James Frobisher before the rest of the family knew he existed. James, who was in the process of converting the place into a workshop, paused for a moment to find a small boy with a mop of dark hair framed in the doorway.

'Hi,' he said. 'Like to come in and have a look?'

The inside was cavernous, and seemed to Luke to be full of planks and woodshavings and nothing much else. An elderly man climbed down from a stepladder and Luke recognized him as Bert Roach, the carpenter who had helped renovate the Old Rectory.

'Why, it's young Luke,' Bert remarked. 'What are *you* doing this far from home?'

'Exploring,' Luke said guardedly. 'Are you making a

proper room in here?' he asked James.

James explained his plan and how it would be when he had finished, as if Luke were an adult and fully cognizant of the restoration of antique furniture. After a while he glanced at his watch and then at Luke.

'It's nearly lunchtime,' he said. 'I think perhaps you should go home now before your mother starts to worry about you.'

'That's right,' Bert Roach agreed. 'So you should.'

Luke tugged at James's hand and pulled him down from his six foot four inches so that he could whisper in his ear. 'I can't do that. I've run away.'

'I see.' James straightened up. 'Are you hungry?' he asked.

Luke nodded.

'Then how about I cut you and me and Bert some sandwiches, and then we talk about it? You can help me.'

In the cottage kitchen, Luke's job was to butter the slices of bread while James laid ham and cucumber on top and cut them in half. The kitchen had a black beam running the length of the ceiling and a pine dresser with blue and white china on the shelves and hooks. Luke became more engrossed with his surroundings than the buttering and the bread kept crumbling, but James did not seem to mind the untidy result. Bert came and collected his lunch, together with a large tin of lager, and retired to the barn again, while James poured himself a beer and a glass of Coke for Luke before they sat down at the scrubbed wooden table to eat.

'I know it's none of my business,' James said, 'but are you going to tell me who you are and why you've run away?'

Luke looked at him warily. 'My name is Luke Stavely

125

and I live in the Old Rectory, and Daddy won't listen to me or let me join in. He does things all the time with Cass, but not with me; he says I'm too young, but that's just an excuse. He doesn't like me, he only likes Cass.' He carefully tucked a piece of escaping ham between the slices of bread and took a bite. 'That's why I've run away,' he concluded through his sandwich.

James listened seriously to this account of blatant favouritism before saying, 'How about your mother? I bet she wants you: mothers are usually keen on sons.'

Luke kept his eyes on his plate. 'Mum's really nice,' he said without elaborating.

'Don't you think she's going to be terribly worried about you then?' James asked gently.

Luke's eyes shot up to stare at James, his thin face turning pink. 'I left her a note,' he announced defensively. 'I told her I would be all right and I was going to see Cleo in London.'

'Who's Cleo?'

'My aunt.'

'It costs money to travel. Have you got any?'

Luke stuck a hand in the pocket of his jeans and drew out a collection of coins. 'Three pounds and sixty pence,' he said, laying them on the table. 'Is that enough?'

'I'm afraid not. And I still believe your mother is worried sick about you.' James poured out the last of his beer. 'Listen, I've a proposition to put to you,' he said.

'A – what?'

'A suggestion. If you telephone your mother now to put her mind at rest, and you let me take you home, you can help me from time to time in my workshop. How's that?'

Luke thought hard. 'Can I do some real carpentry stuff?' he asked.

'As long as you do exactly as I say, yes.'

'Daddy's going to be furious.'

James got to his feet. 'I've a feeling he won't be once it's been explained to him. The telephone's over here. Do you know the number or shall I look it up?'

The moment Ellie put down the receiver, she realized that she should not have accepted James Frobisher's offer to bring Luke home on his way into Stourton. After all, she knew nothing about him, and had she not warned the children never to accept lifts from strangers? She therefore went through a second agonizing quarter of an hour before his Land Rover ground to a halt in her driveway and Luke darted into her arms, apparently unharmed.

'Please don't ever do that to me again,' she told him without anger, and lifting a face pale from recent anxiety to James, 'I'm terribly grateful to you for looking after him. Thank you,' she said.

'It was no trouble.'

'Won't you come in and have some coffee or a drink?'

'Thank you, but I'd better push on. I'll leave you both alone; Luke's got some explaining to do.'

'Yes, he certainly has.' Ellie squeezed Luke's shoulder. 'Say thank you to Mr Frobisher,' she said.

'Thanks a lot. When can I come and help you?' Luke asked.

'I'll give you a call. That's a promise. If your mother agrees, that is.'

'You're newly moved in, aren't you?' Ellie enquired. 'You must come and see us; come to supper perhaps.'

'I'd like that.'

'I don't know where you live, or your telephone number.'

He found a card in the inside pocket of his jacket and handed it to her, said a brief goodbye and turned to go. He knew, as he drove away, that his manner must have seemed abrupt; but the truth was that Ellie Stavely had reminded him disconcertingly of his ex-wife. It was not so much her appearance, although the honey-coloured hair and the slight build were similar, but more her mannerisms, the way she gestured with her hands. Sonia had not been part of his life for two years now, and he did not exactly mind the similarity, but it had taken him aback and brought on an attack of the acute shyness of which he had never quite managed to rid himself.

Ellie was too fraught from the nightmare of Luke's disappearance to gain more than a passing impression of James Frobisher: a gentle self-effacing man who had done her a kindness, was the opinion she was left with. Hardly glancing at his card, she had left it on the hall table for future reference while she tried to discover from Luke the reason for his behaviour. To make it less of an interrogation she gave him a helping of rhubarb crumble and they sat at the garden table in the early September sunshine. She need not have worried; far from being averse to explaining, it all came tumbling out of him without hesitation. It did not surprise her that his complaints stemmed from Philip's lack of attention; his preference for Cass had been obvious from the day Luke was born. She had made endless excuses to herself for Philip's attitude: the sleepless nights of Luke's babyhood, the toddler tantrums, the disruption to Philip's work. But those days were over and still he persisted in brushing Luke aside in favour of Cass. Luke's musical ability, instead of being a source of pride to Philip, merely proved a further irritant. Piano practise was tolerated, but Luke was banished to the top of the house with his violin; and Ellie's attempts to get Philip to show some enthusiasm, or produce a few words of praise for him, generally failed. Watching him now, spooning up the pudding, long dark eyelashes feathering his cheeks, so like Philip and yet poles apart, she was flooded with a protective instinct and anger at Philip for what she saw as gross unfairness.

'Why did you choose Cleo to run to?' she asked Luke, genuinely curious. Cleo, Alex's childless wife, seemed a strange choice.

'Because she's kind and I thought she'd understand,' Luke answered, scraping the bowl.

'You could have told *me* you were miserable,' Ellie said, wounded. '*I* understand.'

'But I didn't know that, did I? You might have taken Daddy's side.'

It was said matter-of-factly, but the words underlined all the vulnerability of being a child.

'Where is he?' Luke asked.

'He's gone to the railway station at Stourton in case you had taken the bus there.'

'Will he be *very* angry?'

'No,' Ellie promised firmly. 'No, he certainly will not; not when I've talked to him. Besides,' she added, 'to be fair, he gets impatient rather than furious.'

'I s'pose Cass is with him,' Luke said gloomily.

'She's gone to Betsy's house to play with Hilary,' Ellie told him, glad that this was one occasion when Cass was not trailing round with Philip. She removed the empty rhubarb-crumble bowl and crouched down to Luke's level. 'Promise me that next time you have a problem, you'll come to me with it,' she said, and he nodded.

The episode had produced a full-scale but short-lived row between Philip and Ellie, in which she had had the upper hand. He had returned from a fruitless search for his son to find him in the garden constructing a bow and arrow. Philip had been badly shaken by Luke's disappearance, and relief at his safety turned to anger. He swept past Ellie in the kitchen in the direction of the back door.

'The little so-and-so is going to have a piece of my mind,' he muttered in passing.

'Don't you dare!' Ellie brandished the knife she was using to chop vegetables. 'It's your fault he went missing in the first place.'

He stopped in his tracks. 'For God's sake, Ellie, put that down before you do one of us an injury.'

For the next ten minutes battle ensued across the kitchen table while she accused him of insensitivity and wilful neglect of his son amounting to cruelty. Later, feeling she had perhaps gone too far, she withdrew the cruelty charge. But Ellie when roused was formidable, all flashing eyes and clenched fists, and never more so than when defending her young. Philip, who hated confrontation and avoided it wherever possible, parried the accusations ineffectually for a certain time and then, sinking onto a chair, raised placating hands in the air and called for a truce.

'All right. So I'm a rotten father, but I'm not a monster. Don't you think you're overreacting? Luke also, if it comes to that.'

'Children don't work like that. They don't run away for no reason; he was miserable.'

130

'It was rather a theatrical gesture, drawing attention to himself.'

'Exactly; the attention you've failed to give him,' Ellie retorted, pouncing on his unwise statement. 'I simply don't understand how you can give Cass all the time in the world and leave him out.'

He heaved a sigh. If anything was theatrical, she thought with irritation, it was his sighs.

'It wasn't intentional,' he said. 'I suppose the truth is that Cass, at nearly eleven, is more interesting than Luke at seven. One can have quite deep conversations with her and I find that intriguing.'

Ellie picked up the knife again and chopped a carrot in quick, expert rat-a-tat-tats. 'If you put the least effort into a conversation with Luke, you might find him equally rewarding,' she told him shortly. 'You could start now while Cass happens to be elsewhere.'

'Stop organizing me, Ellie,' he said quietly. 'You've made your point; just let me get on with things in my own way and in my own time. OK?' He got to his feet and opened the fridge. 'Is there anything to eat? I've missed lunch,' he added pointedly.

One could push Philip so far and no further, as she well knew. They spoke little for the rest of the day until the evening. From the bedroom window she could see him in the orchard with Luke, experimenting with the bow and arrow; Philip had made a paper target and nailed it to an apple tree. Later he told Luke a bedtime story about a dinosaur, a long and complicated one incorporating many different voices, as Ellie could hear during the washing of Cass's hair. It was a good beginning.

The atmosphere between them had thawed out before supper. She came to him where he was sitting and twined her arms round his neck.

'I'm sorry I called you cruel,' she said. 'I take it back. I was so worried . . .'

He kissed her. 'About my neglect?' he suggested. 'There was some truth in that, probably.'

'I didn't want Luke to miss out on affection as you did with your father,' she said. 'You know, the pattern repeating itself from one generation to another.'

'Good God!' He looked at her in horror. 'Surely you're not comparing Luke's childhood with mine? A tyrannical father and a mother who wouldn't have my hair cut until I was six? It would be difficult to reach such heights of parental insanity as theirs. We have to be doing better than them, however inept.'

'*We* are,' Ellie said. 'But then, I had a sane and happy upbringing. I have a sneaking fondness for your mother, but I have to admit that Hugh is a dreadful old man. Which reminds me; it's our turn to have them for Christmas this year.'

'We could bribe Alex and Cleo to take them on.'

'I doubt it,' she said. 'Talking of owing people, we must have James Frobisher to supper to say thank you. I'll have to find someone to ask with him.'

'You haven't described him.'

'Fortyish, very tall, likeable.' But when she tried to put a face to him, her mind went a blank.

With seven major film successes behind him, it had seemed as if Philip could do no wrong; he was arguably the actor of his generation most in demand on either side of the Atlantic. By 1986 he was in a position to pick and choose from the offers that his agent consistently had lined up for him, and restless by nature, he was looking for a part with a difference, a

132

challenge of some kind. He was convinced he had found what he was searching for in a script involving a young girl's obsession with a Catholic priest and set in contemporary Ireland. His agent, Willie Gilmour, advised him against it and worked hard to make him change his mind; the theme was banal, he claimed, and the director was far from happy about his assignment. Philip would be wise to forget it. But the part of the priest had caught his imagination and he refused to be dissuaded; filming eventually went ahead.

Ellie, who had a great deal of respect for Willie Gilmour and his opinions, also wondered at the wisdom of Philip's decision. A fleeting premonition of trouble crossed her mind like a cloud over the sun. Another matter had been occupying her thoughts recently; she would be thirty-six the following year and her child-bearing years were numbered. Cass and Luke were both at school and she wanted another baby while she still had the energy. Philip had been filming for a month in Ireland when she had discovered that she was pregnant with Harriet, and she flew over for a weekend to share the news with him. It was a worrying three days. She found him on edge; there had been problems with the main photography owing to bad weather, they were running behind schedule and the girl playing opposite him was an unknown fresh from rep and nervous as a kitten. He received the news of Ellie's pregnancy with delight and his special brand of sweetness, gathering her in his arms in a bear-hug and telling her how clever she was. But once the excitement had worn off, he became distant again and the worry lines between his eyes knotted up. Judging by two of their evenings spent in the pub with other members of the cast, it struck her that he was drinking more than usual, and she returned home fighting off a bout of anxiety. He had taken on this part against everybody else's better judgement and the strain was beginning to show. To counteract these disturbing thoughts, she threw herself into planning the refurbishment of the nursery where Luke still slept; he would have to be moved to the small spare room next to Cass to make room for the baby. With colour charts and drawers full of cast-off baby clothes, she wiled away Philip's absence.

The upheaval in their lives happened with all the unexpectedness of a natural catastrophe. Once he had finished filming, they had taken a ten-day holiday to help him unwind, and on their return, Willie Gilmour had several offers on hand for him. One of these, the lead in a prestigious production with American backing based on a bestselling novel, Willie was particularly anxious for Philip to accept. It was to have as its director one Jerry Waldorf, known for his brilliance as well as his sarcasm and uncertain temper. The production had a great deal of advance publicity; tipped to be film of the year, it was Oscar material, and an Oscar had so far eluded Philip on more than one occasion when he had justly deserved it. This time he followed Willie's advice and allowed himself to be signed up. Work on the new project was due to begin in the spring of 1987, and it so happened that the previous film was released a week beforehand. It turned out to be a cultural and financial disaster.

Philip had been living with his misgivings; the film had had its difficulties. He had imagined mixed notices, a divergence of opinions. He was not prepared for the universal castigation by the critics not only of the production as a whole, but of his performance in particular. He was torn apart: 'Tasteless tale of an Irish Lolita in which Philip Stavely plays the part of a priest with a curious lack of conviction', 'Where is the Philip Stavely who has given us an unforgettable Hamlet?', 'Philip Stavely plays the priest with an embarrassing mixture of lechery and whimsy', 'His performance as an avuncular religious lech does not become Philip Stavely', 'It is sad to see one of our finest actors let himself down in this appalling fiasco.' Philip, who had refused to believe the glittering reviews of the past, believed only too well in these barbed criticisms, and took them to heart. He appeared to bear them with a tight-lipped stoicism that Ellie found more unnerving than all the ranting and roaring in which he normally indulged. She tried hiding the newspapers, claiming to have thrown them away by mistake, but it was no use, he merely went out and bought every publication he could find in order to punish himself. The week before he was due to start work was one of torture; nothing that Ellie said or did to alleviate his depression had any effect. At some point in the middle of it he went up to London for a meeting with Willie Gilmour and came back rather more cheerful, but Ellie could tell it was an alcohol-induced confidence which would not last, and she was right.

The increased drinking worried her. Towards the end of the week she stopped being understanding and accused him of defeatism while helping him to pack.

'For heaven's sake, darling, everyone's allowed one mistake. It's not the be-all and end-all of your career: think positive. You've collared probably the best part of the film year. That's what you'll be remembered for;

the flop will be forgotten in a few weeks' time. Do you really need four pairs of red socks?'

'I don't know, put them in anyway.' He threw a pile of shirts on the bed, sat down on the end of it and put his head in his hands.

'I'm scared, Ellie,' he said. 'I've lost faith in myself.'

She dropped the socks in the suitcase and went to sit beside him. 'No you haven't,' she said emphatically. 'It'll all come back to you once filming starts. You don't know how to act badly.'

'Oh really?' he replied with laboured sarcasm. 'Read any good reviews lately?'

She took him by the arms and shook him. 'Stop it!' she said. 'All this negative thinking is getting you nowhere; it's making me really angry. You're going to make this part the best thing you've ever done, d'you hear me?'

'Yeah! Yeah! What a bully you are.' He pulled her close and kissed her gently on the mouth. 'Let's leave the sodding packing and have a drink.'

'And that's another thing,' she began.

'I know. I'll cut down. I promise.'

On the Saturday she drove him to Heathrow – the greater portion of the film was to be shot in Tuscany. His face as he said goodbye to her was drawn, and she had a miserable feeling of guilt, as if she were sending her child away to school.

'Come and join me there soon. Swear?' he said.

'As soon as I can fix it with Mum and Betsy,' she told him.

She was never to know whether the account he gave her of the ten weeks of filming was the full story. She had always felt there was a piece missing; but then it must have been difficult for him to describe every single nuance of the psychological warfare which broke out between himself and his director, Jerry Waldorf. Ellie was prevented from seeing for herself; three days before she was due to fly out to him, Cass developed chickenpox, followed by Luke a fortnight later. According to Philip, the first two weeks of work ran comparatively smoothly, and after that the situation began to go badly wrong. Jerry Waldorf started to interfere constantly with his interpretation of the part, ordering take after take to correct some imaginary imperfection. Philip, who had normally enjoyed good relationships with his directors, knew when he was being victimized and fought back. The result was a series of bitter arguments, and on more than one occasion a full-scale row. No-one in the cast found Waldorf easy to work with, and they supported Philip's morale as best they could. Rumours ran rife amongst them as to the reasons for Waldorf's attitude; he was homosexual, and it was widely believed that he had wanted his lover for the lead in the production, but had been unable to dissuade the producer from handing the part to Philip. Philip kept the key factor to himself, that Waldorf, within the first few days of filming, had made a sexual suggestion to him and had been turned down, Philip having walked out on him in the restaurant where it took place.

Perhaps, if his morale had been higher, Philip would have handled the clash of personalities from a position of strength. Following, as it had, so closely on the heels of the previous disaster which had seriously undermined him, he found himself living on his nerves. He reached the dangerous stage of needing a drink before work started for the day, and out of a desire for comfort rather than lust, had a brief affair

137

with the actress who played his screen partner. Three days before filming was due to finish, on location in England, Waldorf accused him of being drunk on set. 'You're pissed!' he had said. 'Get out and sober up.'

Something in Philip snapped. 'I'm going for good and you can stuff your fucking picture.' Work was suspended while first Waldorf and then Philip were closeted with the producer, who was tough and to the point.

'Break your contract now and you're finished,' he was told. 'Come off it, Philip, are you *trying* to ruin yourself? Swallow your grievances, get out there and act. What's three days to you, for Christ's sake?'

The film had been completed and in the fullness of time had won awards. Philip, against all odds, had produced a laudable performance. It had not, however, won him an Oscar; doubtless Waldorf, working behind the scenes, had made sure of that. He returned to Ellie a stone lighter than when he had left, with dark lines under his eyes and a tremor in his hands. His homecoming was not exactly a happy one. He made the mistake of confessing his infidelity to Ellie to ease his conscience, which diminished her sympathy for him considerably. She felt the baby kick inside her as he told her, as if in protest at her hurt and anger. Two months went by without any effort on his part to pursue further work. Whenever Willie Gilmour phoned with a list of possibilities, he wriggled out of making a commitment; Ellie caught snatches of his ends of the conversations, giving his health as an excuse. He had become subdued, and spent his time going for long walks and helping her in the kitchen, turning himself into quite a good cook. All these activities were so unlike him that Ellie began to be anxious; but every time she mentioned his working future, he closed up like a clam.

There came a day when Philip was out and she answered the telephone to Willie Gilmour. Philip was wanted for a television play, just the thing, according to Willie, to ease him back into work. He asked solicitously after Philip as though he were convalescent. It was not until the evening, after the children were in bed, that she asked him whether he had rung Willie and come to a decision. He was sitting in an armchair, leaning forward with his arms resting on his knees, turning a glass round and round between his hands.

'I *have* come to a decision,' he said, carefully avoiding her eyes, 'but it's not the one you mean.'

She waited in silence.

'I've known for some time; I'd have told you before, but I didn't know how to.' He took a deep breath. 'I'm bringing my career to an end. I'm finished with acting.'

She stared at him in disbelief. 'But why?' she asked, bewildered. 'It's your life; you're at the top. Why give up now?'

'I haven't any choice,' he answered. 'It's given *me* up; I've lost my nerve. I can't get myself in front of a camera without a couple of vodkas inside me.'

With a queer choking noise that might have been construed as a laugh, he started to cry, fumbling in his pocket for a handkerchief. Ellie, her bitterness over the affair blotted out, dropped onto her knees beside him and laid her cheek against his.

'It *will* come back,' she said. 'You've had a bad run and you need rest, but it *will* come back.'

But he had merely shaken his head wordlessly, and she had a sudden and frightening preconception of the end of their world as she knew it.

Chapter 6

On the third day of the holiday, Luke left his room in the lower half of the villa and climbed the steps in search of breakfast. He could smell coffee as he neared the open door to the kitchen, and guessed that Cleo was there, just as she had been at eight o'clock on the two previous mornings. They had breakfasted together on the terrace, not from any preconceived plan but simply because their waking hours appeared to coincide. She was a creature of routine, and in his present mood, Luke found this trait oddly reassuring. He admired the way in which she had organized their arrival as they stood around rather helplessly, travel-stained and weary and surrounded by luggage. Cleo had done her homework on the interior of the Villa Sophia and, knowing exactly where everyone was to sleep, had allocated the bedrooms with all the competence of a first-class travel rep. Luke, catching a look of irritation on his mother's face, realized that she did not share his appreciation of Cleo's leadership qualities. But then, there was little to be done about them; from the outset the holiday was bound to be in Cleo's hands.

He found her standing at the kitchen table, wearing a white cotton shift and slicing a long loaf into portions.

'Hallo there,' she said, turning her shiny early morning face to smile at him. 'We meet again; the first ones up as usual.'

He gave her a peck on the cheek. 'Shall I take the cups and things through to the terrace?'

'Yes, please. I'll follow with the coffee.'

On the terrace he laid out the cups and plates on the round table where they had their meals, and went to lean his arms on the wrought-iron railing. Below him, and beyond the silver-leaved olive trees, was the deep improbable blue of the sea, and to the right, the mile-long beach executed a gentle curve to a distant promontory. The far end was the crowded part, close to the two tavernas and water-sports centre. The stretch of beach closer to home was miraculously empty of all but families like themselves holidaying in the nearby villas. The terrace, which ran all the way round the Villa Sophia, was partially shaded from the sun by wooden slats with a vine entwined between them and decorated with troughs of geraniums. The villa was built on two floors; Luke and Cass had the two garden bedrooms with a shower room between them, and the rest of their party were distributed above them where the bedrooms led off a huge living room. A narrow path wound its way down through the olive grove to a cluster of flat rocks and a short stone jetty with a sailing dinghy moored at its end. At this hour of the morning a sprinkler was already spraying the oleanders, and the scent of rosemary drifted up from the little garden to mingle with the smell of coffee and warm bread. While Luke's senses noted these pleasing details, he thought of Hilary Groves.

'There we are,' Cleo said, unloading a coffee pot, a basket of bread, butter and honey from her tray.

They ate in companionable silence until she had refilled their coffee cups.

'What are your plans for today?' she asked.

'I haven't thought. I expect I'll walk along the beach and have another go at windsurfing.' He grinned. 'I couldn't get upright on the bloody thing yesterday, but I might as well try. The trouble is it's expensive.'

'Let me stand you a lesson.'

He flushed. 'God, no. Thank you, but you're doing enough for us as it is.'

'Nonsense.' She sipped her coffee. 'The important thing is for everyone to enjoy themselves. I only hope your mother will be able to relax,' she remarked thoughtfully. 'She's very tense at the moment.'

'It's not easy for her,' he said, sensing criticism. 'She's having to get used to doing things without Pa for the first time.'

'It's hard on all of you,' Cleo replied.

'Worse for her, though.'

'I'm going to suggest she helps Alex with the food shopping this morning.' She brushed crumbs from her lap with a brisk gesture. 'A bit of male company can have a therapeutic effect, and whatever else Alex is, he is calming.'

Silently Luke queried the therapeutic effect of a morning spent in a Greek supermarket. 'Oh, right,' he agreed vaguely.

'And you, Luke; I worry that you're without anyone of your own age, that you may get bored.'

'There's Cass,' he pointed out.

'Yes,' she said doubtfully, 'but she's not very *active*, if you know what I mean.'

'I'm not in the least bored.'

'You could have brought a friend; I hope you know that. A girlfriend, if you have one.' She glanced at him, rather obviously expecting an answer.

He did not find her probing intrusive; in fact he was

142

quite pleased to talk about Hilary. 'There's someone I've been seeing quite a lot of,' he said. 'She's a medical student. But she's not exactly a girlfriend. As yet,' he added.

It had taken a certain amount of courage to telephone a girl he had only met once on a train. The fact that they had known each other as children did not count; he could not remember her. When he finally rang her hall of residence, it was to find she had moved to a flat which she was sharing with three others. She sounded unsurprised on the phone, as if she had been expecting to hear from him, and they arranged to meet when he had weekend leave from school. He had gone to her flat in Maida Vale and got lost on the way, eventually finding it in a gloomy Edwardian block wedged between a laundry and a National Car Park. The flat itself had been divided into several small rooms with high ceilings, and was cluttered with unwashed mugs, medical text books and various discarded pieces of outdoor clothing. Hilary's flatmates, two men and a girl, were watching television when he arrived; Hilary introduced him and whisked him into the kitchen.

'We can either stay in and all eat a takeaway,' she said, 'or you and I can go out and be private. Which do you want?'

He hesitated. 'I'd rather it was just us,' he said. 'The problem is, I don't have much cash on me.'

'We'll have a pizza and go Dutch,' she answered. 'There's a Pizza Hut round the corner.'

The place was crowded, but they managed to find the last table for two. After swift mental arithmetic he ordered a glass of red wine each, and while they ate he studied her surreptitiously to see if she had changed. In place of the baggy sweater she was wearing a big white shirt over a long ethnic skirt, otherwise nothing about her had altered. Every so often she pushed her glasses onto the top of her head and he was diverted by the amazing blue of her eyes. They talked about her gran and his mother, his final term at school and the impending finale to her first year in medical school. She insisted on buying them a second round of wine, and went on to describe a post mortem, but he begged her to stop as it made him queasy. Time passed unnoticed; he felt as though he had known her for ever, which in a sense was true.

'Have you given up on drugs?' she asked him.

He made a face. 'You make it sound like a real crime. It was only pot. Anyway, the answer's yes.'

'Good,' she said. 'A boy died in hospital last week from an overdose of Ecstasy.'

'You'll make a great doctor,' he complained. 'They're always full of dire warnings.'

'I was only pointing out what can happen,' she replied. 'Being caring.'

'OK, but can we talk about something more cheerful. What are you doing in the holidays?'

'I'll have to get a job for some of the time. After that, don't know, haven't thought. How about you?'

He told her about the Corfu villa. 'Come too,' he said on the spur of the moment. 'Cleo won't mind.'

'I can't,' she told him. 'That's when I'll be working. I'm saving up to go to India.'

'That's where I want to go,' he said eagerly. 'I hope to fit it in before going to college.'

'You're spoiled, aren't you?' she said without rancour. 'First Greece and then India. It's all right for some.'

'Greece is a freebie,' he answered defensively. 'But I suppose I *am* lucky – Mum's helping out with the other trip. It'd be great if we could go together,' he added carelessly, and waited for her reaction.

'It won't be this year for me,' she said. 'I haven't a hope of getting the fare together.'

He had been staying the night with Cleo and Alex on that occasion, but he had not mentioned Hilary's name to them; seeing a film with a friend, he told them. There was no real reason to keep Hilary a secret, but he did not particularly want to answer the inevitable questions that would follow. He did not know which way their friendship was going, and he sensed that any interference might spoil it. It was the first time he had had a girlfriend and there were no past experiences with which to compare it. It felt too comfortable for it to be love, inextricably bound up in his mind with sex; and yet he could not stop thinking about her. During his half-term she came down to Darlingford to see her mother, and part of the time he spent with her in London, sleeping on her sofa in the chaotic living room. In the evenings, when she was not working, they went to Kew Gardens or the cinema, and ate cheaply in pubs. He wondered what she would say if he suggested they went to bed together; but instinct told him the time was not right, and besides, it was difficult to find the privacy with her flatmates around. Clarrie, the other girl amongst them, always seemed to be there, as if waiting rather hopelessly to be included in whatever was happening.

And then at last the term had come to an end. His mandatory schooling was finished, and he was left, all of a sudden, a novice in an adult's world. There was a week before the family were to go to Corfu, a week in

145

which he saw Hilary just once. They went by boat to Hampton Court and mingled with the tourists, exploring the palace and the grounds. While in the maze, she told him that she was going to India after all; her mother and her gran, who both had a bit of money put by, had clubbed together to make the trip possible, and she was going with Clarrie.

'Why Clarrie?' he asked, knocked sideways with disappointment.

'Because she needs taking out of her environment to see how the other half lives,' Hilary explained. 'I feel sorry for her. Her parents are loaded, but overprotective. Clarrie doesn't know the meaning of adventure.'

'I wanted us to go together,' Luke insisted obstinately.

'We still could, the three of us,' she suggested. 'Why don't you come too?'

'I wanted it to be the two of us, you and me.'

She stood for a moment in silence, gazing up at the tall dark greenery of the maze, her thin shoulders showing through the fabric of her shirt.

'I don't think I'm ready to get involved yet,' she said eventually. 'There're things I want to do first. Maybe it'll be good for us to have a month or so apart.'

He related a potted version of these events to Cleo, knowing he could rely on her for an unbiased opinion. His mother knew about Hilary, but his inhibitions where she was concerned still prevailed. He could not bring himself to discuss any intimate details of his life with her; and besides, this holiday was for her benefit. There was a tacit agreement amongst them all that she would not be bothered with anyone else's problems while it lasted. Cleo drained her coffee cup and looked at him over the remains of breakfast.

'It sounds as though you've been rushing things,' she remarked. 'Some girls, Hilary being one of them I should imagine, need more wooing. They don't like being bulldozed into a relationship.'

He ran a hand through his hair. 'Then how do you ever – you know – take things a stage further?'

'There will be a right moment; you'll know when it happens. And hang on to the friendship; it lasts. Alex and I are prime examples of that,' she said with confidence. 'And now I'm going to wash up and get on down to the rocks for a little judicious sunbathing.' She bent over to kiss him. 'Cheer up. Write to her, why don't you?'

Provisions for the villa were shopped for at a supermarket called F&M, known as Fortnum and Mason by the English contingent on the island. It stood in the middle of nowhere on the route to Corfu town, and stocked just about everything a household could possibly need, from Calor gas to fresh octopus. Packed off by Cleo, clutching a shopping list, shortly after breakfast, Alex and Ellie trawled the shelves with their trolley, stocking up the larder for the next few days. Ellie had not particularly wanted the assignment. She had slept badly and realized, from the moment she woke, that it was going to be one of those mornings when loss of Philip coloured everything. Tears had trickled from beneath her closed lids, to be hurriedly blinked away when Harriet came to sit on her bed, and her head throbbed. She wondered whether these aching spasms of loneliness would ever stop. Hidden behind dark glasses, she tried to put on a cheerful front for Alex as they discussed what to buy. Having him to herself did nothing to dispel her depression; in a way it worsened it, for he was on loan to her for an hour or two, only under-lining her aloneness. Sending them off together had obviously been one of Cleo's well-intentioned ges-tures; why then, she asked herself, should she feel manipulated?

By the time they had finished the shopping and loaded the back of the hire car with carrier bags and crates of bottled water, it was eleven fifteen. The sun was high in the sky and they drove homeward with every window lowered to catch what breeze there was. Her efforts at brightness had not deceived Alex; he was acutely conscious of her unhappiness. He had been looking forward to three weeks in her company with a mixture of trepidation and anticipation. Now he silently questioned the wisdom of such a scheme; if it gave her no pleasure, there was not much point to it. Perhaps he should have remembered that in this year of Philip's death she was having to do many things without him for the first time; holidays might well increase her sense of isolation. He wished that he had not begun to love her so deeply, that he did not long to stop the car, hold her close and kiss the pain from her face. Uncomfortably he shifted in the seat, the warm fabric prickling his bare legs where his shorts ended, and tried to think of a diversion that might lighten her mood. Halfway along the twisting white road to home there was a small taverna on their left with 'BAR' painted in black on one of the walls. He slowed down and brought the car to a halt, saying, 'I don't know about you, but I'm thirsty.'

She looked worried. 'I ought to get back really, Alex. I've left Cass in charge of Harriet on the beach.'

'Half an hour longer won't do either of them any

harm,' he pointed out cheerfully. 'I think we've earned ourselves a drink.'

She gave in. They climbed the steep steps to the taverna and sat at one of the green tin tables in the shade of a vine. Below them in the distance lay the coastline, dotted here and there with clusters of white houses, and beyond, a dark-blue sea banded inshore with aquamarine. Ellie pushed her dark glasses to the top of her head and gazed with tired eyes.

'It's incredibly beautiful,' she murmured.

'One of the best bits of the island, so they say,' he said. 'Mercifully lacking in the discos and fast-food joints of the built-up areas.'

A young girl brought them mineral water, two glasses of ouzo and dishes of olives and goat's cheese. They added water to the ouzo and watched it grow cloudy. 'This will make me drunk,' she said. 'I didn't have much breakfast.'

'I know. I was there. Eat something now.' He pushed the dishes towards her. 'Oh, Ellie,' he said quietly. 'What can I do about your sadness?'

She glanced up at him and away. 'Nothing,' she said. 'You weren't meant to notice; I'm sorry.'

'Is it being here that's causing it? Are you regretting coming?'

'No, no,' she told him quickly. 'I just get the occasional bad day; it'll pass. Where I happen to be makes no difference.'

This was not strictly true. Alex's and Cleo's marriage might not be ideal, but she envied them. In spite of their kindness, she felt the odd one out, that awkward appendage, a widowed relative; not only an object of pity but something of a threat to their balanced existence, however innocent.

'You mustn't feel under an obligation to be constantly bright and sparkling,' he said, as if he had read her thoughts. 'No-one expects it. All I hope is that you find a little tranquillity while you're here.'

She smiled at him over the rim of her glass. 'Dear Alex.'

'I miss Philip, too, you know. Not in the same way you do, obviously, but we were close, especially as children.' He sipped his ouzo. 'I miss that dry sense of humour of his; he could always make me laugh.'

She sighed. 'There wasn't much sign of it in those last months,' she said. 'He seemed to lose the knack of being funny.' She paused, then added, 'I'd find his dying easier to bear if he hadn't stopped loving me.'

Alex's nice ordinary features creased in sympathy. 'Are you really so convinced he had?'

'I found the evidence I was looking for,' she answered. 'Half a dozen postcards and an unfinished letter, all unsigned. They shouldn't have come as a suprise; I realized he must be having an affair, but all the same I was shaken.'

She fell silent and he waited for her to go on, watching the shadows on her face cast by the vine.

'I thought I'd feel relief if I knew for certain,' she continued, 'but they told me so little: no name, no postcodes, no dates. Only the letter actually made sense. Whoever wrote it was bringing the affair to an end in anguish; you could tell this wasn't a brief unimportant fling. Perhaps the fact that she was leaving him would explain Philip's obvious misery. But then he hadn't been at peace for a long time; I believe he was being tortured by an impossible situation.' She lifted her head to stare unseeingly into the distance. 'If she meant so much to him,' she said, 'why didn't he

150

tell me and ask me for a divorce? I don't understand.'

'Maybe that's not what he wanted,' he suggested. 'Few men can face an entire upheaval in their lives when it comes down to it.'

'It's a negative reason for sticking to a marriage,' she said sadly. 'Last Christmas', she added, remembering, 'he became a different person, changing back into the old Philip. It was as if he had come to a decision and a great load had been lifted from him as a result. He was quieter than he used to be, but he tried terribly hard to make a success of Christmas. It was like a miracle; I thought he had returned to me. I know now what he had decided, of course.'

He took one of her hands in his and gripped it firmly. 'Ellie, you must try to put it all behind you,' he told her. 'Face the fact that you may never know the reason why. Even tragedy has to fade eventually.'

'Even unexplained tragedy?' she said with a query in her voice. 'Somewhere, someone knows the whole story. It makes one wonder what has become of her, and what it feels like to have destroyed a life.'

She sounded curious rather than bitter. He captured her other hand and pulled her round to face him. 'All pain fades,' he insisted, 'but only if you allow it to. Some time you must start to live again instead of merely existing.'

She looked as if she were about to argue; then he felt her hands slacken and saw the tension leave her face. 'You're right, of course,' she said. 'If only I knew how.' Leaning forward, she kissed him on the cheek. 'Thank you, Alex.'

'What on earth for?' he asked.

'Oh, everything. For your patience and your common sense, and just for being there.'

He let go of her hands and reached for his glass, studying the remainder of his drink thoughtfully.

'There is no great virtue in caring for someone you love,' he said.

The words, spoken almost casually, hung in the air between them. How much better, Ellie thought, if they had been left unsaid. She decided to ignore them. Glancing at her watch, she gathered up her shoulder bag and her old straw hat from a spare chair and laid them on her lap.

'Time we were getting back, I think,' she said.

She spoke little in the car, answering Alex's gentle flow of remarks automatically. Her mind kept returning to Cleo, wondering whether she had the least idea of her husband's feelings, and if so, held Ellie responsible. Either way made no difference to Ellie's sense of guilt, which she felt gathering like a storm cloud, as though she and Alex had already entered into an illicit conspiracy.

From her position on the beach, Cass lifted her eyes from her paperback to check on Harriet. Her head, white-blond hair obscured by the snorkel, could be seen cleaving a line through the water, like the wake of an otter, in the direction of the rocks. That was where marine life was to be found. Don't go round the point, Cass had told her; stay where I can see you. Now she waited, a trifle impatiently, to make sure she was being obeyed. A frown creased her forehead without her being aware of it. Normally she would have had no objection to minding Harriet; they had a good relationship. But over the last few months – ever since Philip's death to be accurate – she had developed this weird fixation about her father. It was obvious to

152

Cass that she needed a few sessions with a child psychologist, but Ellie insisted it was just a phase, which was typical, in Cass's scornful opinion, of her mother's blinkered attitude to a problem. In any case, on this particular morning she did not feel inclined to cope with Harriet's fevered imagination. During the night she had had one of her rare dreams about her father and had woken bathed in sweat. The dream, when it did occur, was exactly as her memory had recorded the event, and left her with an awful hollow feeling of betrayal, which lived inside her for the whole of the next day.

She and Harriet had made their encampment close to the sea; an air-bed, towels and a beach umbrella, which Cass pushed precariously into the soft sand.

'We'd better wedge it with stones,' she said. 'Go and fetch a couple, will you, Harry?'

Harriet had taken her time. She wandered back eventually with a stone in each hand, her face flushed. 'There was a man,' she said.

Cass stared at her. Shit! she thought, that's all I need. 'What man? Where?'

Harriet pointed vaguely. 'He was walking along the beach that way, towards the tavernas.' She squatted down to put the stones in place. 'I only saw his back; he looked exactly like Daddy,' she said, squinting into the sun at Cass. 'I called to him, and he turned and then I saw it wasn't.'

'Of course it wasn't.' Cass glared down at her irritably. 'You know you shouldn't speak to strange men, and it's about time you accepted the fact that Daddy's dead. He had an accident; people do. You're ten now, too old for pretending.'

Harriet stared back. Her face crumpled and the tears

welled up and slid down her cheeks. 'You're foul,' she muttered.

'Don't, *please*,' Cass pleaded, hit by remorse. She put her arms round Harriet's thin shoulders and hugged her. 'I *was* foul and I'm sorry. But you do worry me, Harry. Let's forget all about it and go and have a swim. We'll take the Lilo if you like.'

She had found a packet of tissues in her beach bag and mopped up Harriet, and the therapeutic effect of warm sea water had done the rest. The rift was healed. Harriet had remained there with her snorkel and Cass had returned to read and sunbathe. But she found it difficult to concentrate. She was conscious of having gained no brownie points so far in her role as surrogate mother, and last night's dream lingered darkly at the back of her mind. She had just decided that she had had enough sun for one morning, and was preparing to move into the shade of the umbrella when a shadow fell across her book. She quickly fastened her bikini bra strap and sat up to find Walter standing in front of her. Walter was one half of a couple of amiable homosexuals who were staying in a nearby apartment and frequented one of the tavernas in the evening. Cleo had made up her mind that they looked interesting and had gathered them into the family circle for an after-dinner drink. There was nothing particularly camp about either of the two men. Walter was considerably older than his partner Malcolm and his hair was greying becomingly at the temples. He smiled down at Cass and she smiled back stiffly.

'Sorry if I startled you,' he said, squatting beside her. 'Malc and I are having a barbecue tomorrow night on the beach, and I came to ask if you would all like to join us.'

She searched in vain for an excuse. 'It sounds great,' she replied weakly. 'Can we let you know? I'm the only one here at the moment; I'll ask Cleo and Alex at lunchtime.'

'Fine,' he said. 'Hope you can make it.'

She watched him walk away, an unremarkable middle-aged figure. A shiver went through her despite the heat, as if a trickle of iced water was running down her spine. She pulled the air-bed into the shade and slumped on it; Harriet was by the rocks, doubtless hovering over the clusters of sea urchins. Cass, who prided herself, like most of her generation, on her lack of prejudice, felt aware of intolerance towards the harmless Walter which was almost akin to hatred. She despised herself but she could not help it. He had unwittingly forced her to relive her dream at a moment when she had been trying to get rid of it, stuffing it back into her subconscious in the forlorn hope that it would not re-emerge. It was one o'clock in the morning and she was in Dominic Fraser's flat in South Kensington, curled up on the sofa bed in the sitting room. This was how it had been, both in her sleep and in reality. Since he and Dominic were apt to work late, her father spent three or four nights a week at the flat, and Cass was allowed a key on the strict understanding that she telephone first before using it. On this occasion she had been to an impromptu party and missed the last train home to Darlingford; it was after midnight, too late to ring the flat without the possibility of waking one or other of them. She had broken the rules and let herself in; not daring to make the sofa into a bed for fear of being heard moving around, she lay down fully clothed and pulled her coat over her for warmth. The sitting room opened on to the corridor opposite the larger of the two bedrooms where Dominic slept; Philip occupied the single one on the far side of the bathroom. Before drifting asleep, she thought she heard the murmur of voices, but it could have come from the next-door flat. She woke some time later in need of the lavatory and padded blearily across the room, a shaft of light from the full moon guiding her. She opened the door and everything that followed seemed to happen in slow motion. The door to Dominic's room opened simultaneously and her father stood there, wearing only a pair of boxer shorts, his skin pale as a wraith in the moonlight and his dark hair tousled. They stood like statues, their faces blank with mutual shock at the sight of each other. Behind Philip's motionless figure Cass could see one half of a large bed and Dominic's naked arm lying across the bedclothes. Her mind grappled wildly for a reasonable explanation, the obvious and immediate one being too awful to contemplate. Dominic's voice broke the silence, bored and muffled from recent sleep.

'There's a howling draught, Phil. For God's sake shut the door and come back to bed.'

Slowly Philip closed the door, leaving himself in the corridor. He put out a hand towards Cass in a pleading gesture, and for no more than a second she stared into his agonized eyes. Then, brushing his hand aside, she ran stumbling to the lavatory where she was violently sick. She knelt there, gripping the cold rim of the lavatory basin, until the nerves of her stomach were retching on nothing. Philip was knocking softly on the door. 'Cass, are you all right?' She grimaced and flushing the cistern, ran the cold tap of the handbasin and splashed her face with icy water. 'Cass, please answer me. We have to talk.' About what, she thought fiercely? What was there to say? She had discovered her father was gay, and he was expecting her to sit down and have a cosy discussion about it.

'Leave me alone. Please,' she said.

'Very well; we'll talk in the morning. Try to get some sleep.'

She waited until she heard the door to his room close – his own room this time, as if it mattered any longer: the damage was done – before returning to the sitting room on legs that trembled under her. He had put a blanket and pillows on the sofa. She did not sleep. Wrapping herself in the blanket she wept silently and copiously for memories of times past, now muddied beyond redemption; precious moments spent with her father, hearing his lines, listening to the stories he invented, picking primroses in the woods, laughing hysterically at his fund of silly verse. A lot of little girls put their fathers on pedestals, and most fathers had fallen off them by the time their daughters were grown women; Cass knew this. But few men crashed so dramatically in their children's estimation that the cracks could not be mended. The hurt of his betrayal was appalling; it throbbed like a physical injury.

They never talked about it. When the cold grey of a December dawn crept through the windows, she had got up, made herself a cup of tea and let herself out of the flat for the last time. The following weekend Philip had flown to Los Angeles on business and she did not see him for a fortnight. When they met, he behaved as though nothing had happened. Gradually, as the months passed and the initial shock had worn off, and because she still loved him, she was able to make excuses for his deviation. No-one, she told herself, bringing her liberalism into play, could help their sexuality. But her father was not just anyone, and a whole lot of unfocused anger remained in her. It needed an outlet and she made her mother the recipient; never quite believing in Ellie's apparent ignorance of what was happening in her marriage. Cass's resentment stuck, and her churlishness towards her mother had become a habit which, it had to be admitted, she did not try very hard to cure.

Harriet appeared, carrying her snorkel, and flopped down beside her, distributing sand everywhere.

'Is it time for lunch?' she asked hopefully.

James Frobisher unlocked the front door of the Old Rectory with the set of keys left for him by Ellie and bent to pick up the mail. He sorted it into a neat bundle and placed it with the stack already on the hall table, then started on his patrol of the house. He took his responsibilities seriously, particularly so where Ellie was involved; checking for leaky plumbing, insecure window latches and any attempted break-ins, for Darlingford was not without its vandals. Having finished with the ground floor, he made his way upstairs, moving from bedroom to bedroom and ending up in Ellie's, where the double bed faced the window, serene under its unruffled white lace cover. Each time he entered her room he felt as if he were intruding, and his heart gave a little lurch, just as it had lurched when he had first met her twelve years ago. He had only experienced the sensation once before in his life and it had led to marriage; a disastrous one as it turned out. Not that he allowed himself to think of Ellie in terms of anything other than friendship. He had always imagined her and Philip to be totally bound up in each other; and even now, when he knew that all had not been well between them and Philip was dead, he realized that she was in no fit state to embark on a relationship. Besides, she was not interested; one could always tell.

A fly buzzed and bumped against the window panes. He unscrewed the security lock, pushed up the lower sash and brushed the insect out into the warm summer air. In the distance the chalk cart track wound its way up the hill like a white ribbon towards the woods. Out of sight was the exact spot where Philip had died, hidden by the brow of the slope. James wondered, not for the first time, whether Ellie was disturbed by this reminder whenever she looked at the view. Perhaps it would be better for her to have the room rearranged so that the bed did not face directly on to the window, but it was not the kind of question he felt able to ask her. He was always, without being conscious of doing so, thinking of ways in which to help her. Moving slowly towards the doorway, he paused by the walnut chest of drawers, the top of which was clustered with photographs and snapshots. Smiling faces of her family gazed out at him, ignorant of the tragedy that was to overtake them.

He used to be secretly envious of Philip and Ellie, not because of their share of fame and success, but for the close-knit nature of their life together. Their children were an integral part of it; holidays were mostly family ones, discussions were thrown open to them and their points of view listened to. Maybe they were spoiled, James could not say, but it was a way of married life that he had missed out on and regretted. Sonia had been the type of wife who demanded her husband's full attention and flatly refused to allow their only child Susie to become an obstacle to her lifestyle. No bucket-and-spade holidays for Sonia; when she was not dragging James across Europe to villa parties in Italy or the South of France, she was partying in London. If she did not have a full diary she became neurotic. Susie was left in the care of a series of nannies who came and went with monotonous regularity, and it fell to James alone to supply her with love and attention. It was not easy; he was working long hours in those days. But he gave up most of his weekends to be with her, to play games and to teach her to read and to take her to places. She grew into a solemn, clever little girl, inheriting her mother's long slim legs and her parents' blond hair and lashes, and he adored her. The marriage was already on the rocks and Susie was his sole reason for not bringing it to an end. It lasted precisely six months after he was made redundant from his job with an investment firm in the City. Sonia left to live in New York, where she married again to an American lawyer, and Susie went with her. In theory James was allowed reasonable access to his daughter; in practice it was not so simple to ship a child backwards and forwards across the Atlantic. She came once to stay with him when he had just bought the cottage and the barn. It was not a success; she was already urbanized by New York, the country bored her, and the rapport they once had had sadly vanished. The flow of letters she used to write him dried up and even the card at Christmas had ceased. The last he heard was that she was in a rehabilitation clinic for drug and alcohol addiction; so Sonia informed him by letter, pointing out that the exorbitant bill for such treatment was his responsibility.

He took a last look round before going downstairs to the kitchen and opening a tin of cat food. The cat

Mozart made a timely entrance through the flap and wound himself round James's legs, meowing loudly. James was glad of his company; the emptiness of the house depressed him, and he found himself wishing that it was the day of Ellie's return, when he would put flowers in the hall and in her bedroom and anticipate a telephone call from her. His secret dread was that one day she would up-sticks and leave the village for good, unable to live any longer in the shadow of unhappy memories. Understated as their relationship was, he could not now imagine living without her nearby.

'Are we all agreed, then?' Cleo enquired a trifle crisply over lunch. 'Corfu town it is this evening, starting around four o'clock.'

She was getting a little tired, she had decided, of doing all the organizing; if it weren't for her, none of them would get to see anything of interest.

There was a certain tension in the air, the kind of prickliness that often precedes an electric storm, but the weather was clear and unsullied, and the heat dry. Quite simply, they had reached the stage, midway through the holiday, when small clashes of personality and minor irritations had begun to make themselves felt. Ellie wondered if it wouldn't be tactful of her to stay behind on the proposed expedition and give Alex and Cleo a chance to be together without her tagging along, but she knew this would not be popular either. Cleo took pride in her role as entertainments manager, and expected people to fall in with her. One could not win. Besides, Ellie needed to buy presents, little things for her mother and for Betsy Groves.

'Fine,' she said. 'We'll be ready.'

Later she washed up the lunch things with Cass's

help. Lunch was the same each day, consisting of salads, cold meats, cheeses and occasionally a dish of large prawns bought fresh from one of the fishermen down at the taverna. The chore of preparing it and clearing it away was shared out between them in turn. It was not possible for Ellie, with her hands in the sink and her back to the room, to gauge Cass's mood. Conversation was confined mainly to food. 'There's hardly any tomato salad left. Shall I bin it?' Or, 'We're running out of cling film.' It seemed to Ellie that Cass's spirits had lightened in the last few days. She had arrived looking pale and tired after her finals; by now the sun and the sea had brought the colour back, and she had acquired a boyfriend, a Dutch student sharing one of the taverna apartments with three others. Out of all her three children, Ellie worried over Cass the most; Philip's death, it seemed had hit her the hardest. She never mentioned it. Her life at university remained a blank also, although Ellie guessed something or someone, a man presumably, had added to her unhappiness. A wealth of things left unsaid lay between them and Ellie, sensing resentment, had the inexplicable feeling that Cass blamed her for what had happened. She longed to end this enforced separation from her daughter, alternately wanting to hug her or shake her into communicating; always watching for the right moment.

She unplugged the washing-up water and reached for a towel to dry her hands. 'There, that's finished,' she said, smiling at Cass who was wiping the last plate.

'Shall I put this lot away?' she asked.

'Not to worry; I'll do it,' Ellie told her.

'OK, only I want to wash my hair.'

'Are you coming to Corfu town later?'

'I suppose so,' Cass said without enthusiasm. 'I'd quite like to look at the shops. I want to be back by eight thirty, though; Hans and I are going to a disco.'

'I'm glad you've found someone to do things with,' Ellie remarked, starting to put the plates into a cupboard. 'He seems a nice boy; lots of charm.'

Cass's face took on its familiar look of contempt. 'He's a man, Mum, not a boy,' she said.

'I've reached the age when all men under thirty are boys,' Ellie insisted bravely.

'And he's much too straight to be charming,' Cass went on. 'I can't stand charm; it's a form of deception.'

'Can't you?' Ellie replied. 'Then we must agree to differ. I find it brightens life up no end, and I don't mind a little harmless deception.' Why do I bother to open my mouth, she asked herself? 'I'll see you later,' she added dismissively.

'Yeah, OK.' Cass hovered in the open doorway. 'What are you planning to do in the town? Go round the church which Cleo wants to see – or is it the palace?'

'Both, knowing Cleo. I shall probably visit one of them and then do some shopping. Harriet will get bored with sightseeing.'

Cass stifled a yawn and replaced it with a little secret smile. 'No prizes for guessing where Alex will choose to be,' she remarked.

Ellie felt the colour rise in her face. 'Oh, where?'

'Wherever you are, of course.'

Hurriedly she opened a drawer and put away the cutlery with a clatter. She felt Cass's eyes on her. 'I don't know what you mean.'

'Come on, Mum. He makes it pretty obvious, following you around like man's best friend, fussing over you.' Cass sounded amused. 'It's amazing that Cleo hasn't noticed,' she said, 'or doesn't mind; one or the other.'

Ellie slammed the drawer shut and swung round. 'You go too far, Cass,' she said coldly. 'Alex is a kind and a caring man and we owe him a lot. Don't let me catch you spreading rumours about him again.'

It was Cass's turn to flush, taken aback by Ellie's unprecedented attack. She stared down at her bare feet. 'Sorry,' she muttered. 'I wasn't being that serious.'

'In that case,' Ellie snapped, 'it wasn't worth saying.'

Later, when Cass had left in silence, she fetched a book from her room and lay on one of the long chairs on the shaded terrace. But her concentration was poor and she kept lifting her head to stare into the distance, feeling guilty twice over: about Alex, and for losing her temper. The view, the silver-leaved olive trees, the azure sea and the misty coastline beyond that belonged to Albania, was temporarily spoiled for her. A premonition of some kind, of upheaval or disaster, lurked in her mind and refused to be shifted.

Harriet had disappeared. She had been with her mother in a jewellery shop where Ellie was looking at silver bracelets, when she caught sight of her father. She had gone to stand in the open doorway and, parting the bead curtains, had seen Philip passing. There was no mistaking the tall thin figure with the lock of dark hair falling over his forehead, and the pink shirt to which he was particularly attached. Harriet's heart leaped; she had known all along she would find him one day. He was walking with long loping strides, the only one amongst the strolling crowds to be in a hurry. She had slipped from the shop and followed, weaving her way between the people and half running, desperate to keep him in view.

Earlier in the afternoon they had all been to see the church which was dedicated to St Spiridon, the island's patron saint; even Cass had come, who was an agnostic and wasn't really interested. The interior was dark and cool and cavernous and smelled of incense. Harriet had found a plaster effigy of someone she supposed was St Spiridon placed on an altar in a side chapel. His painted face had a sympathetic expression, as if he really cared about people's problems, and she said a silent prayer to him on the spur of the moment, to bring back her father. She doubted if the nuns at school would have approved; one was only meant to pray to God or the Virgin Mary. But the church belonged to the saint in a way, so she could not see any harm in asking him a favour.

They had left the church and stood in a group, blinking in the sudden brightness, and discussed what they were going to do next. Alex and Cleo decided to visit an art gallery and Luke had chosen to go with them. Cass had gone off on her own to look at ethnic clothes. Ellie and Harriet left together to buy presents. It was arranged that they would all meet up at the Café Christos at seven o'clock, close to where Alex had parked the car and overlooking the public gardens near the seafront. Harriet and her mother wandered along narrow streets lined with every type of shop and enclosed between tall buildings bedecked with elegant wrought-iron balconies; a legacy from the Venetian occupation of Corfu, Ellie told Harriet, having read snippets of Cleo's guidebook. They walked in the road since everyone else was doing so; the traffic seemed non-existent, and if a car came, it drove slowly with a blaring of its horn.

At first Harriet had found the shopping quite fun. They bought a blue and yellow pottery jug for James Frobisher, and silver earrings for Betsy Groves. By the third shop, the one with the bracelets, she was growing bored. That was when she left Ellie at the counter and held the bead curtain aside to watch the street scene. She did not think once of her mother as she ran after Philip; there was no thought in her head other than to catch up with him and beg him to come home. However urgent his business in Corfu, surely it couldn't be more important than Ellie and his children? If she could only talk to him, at least she could get him to explain why he had left them.

She could still see him ahead of her, but she was not gaining on him. They had twisted and turned down several streets now, to the right and the left and the right again, the dark head above the pink shirt always at the same distance from her, and she was running out of breath. The evening was warm and she could feel her T-shirt sticking to her back, and the clamminess of her clenched hands. She wished he would slow down, go into a shop for something, so that she would be near enough to call to him. And then, suddenly, they were in a street that she recognized, one that led to the gardens and the seafront; and in the far right-hand corner was the Café Christos, where people were seated outside at the marble-topped tables, drinking their aperitifs. His pace slackened, and to her joy he came to a halt by the café, scanning the tables as if searching for someone. She was very nearly there, very nearly close enough to shout to him, when a woman stood up and waved; not to Harriet but to Philip. He moved over to her and kissed her on both cheeks, and handed her a small bouquet of flowers wrapped in white paper. The woman was tall, almost as tall as he was, with long blond hair, and Harriet could see that she was beautiful. Harriet stared, faltered and felt the excitement of finding her father drain away. Something was wrong; the woman shouldn't be there, holding Philip's arm as though he belonged to her. The dreadful suspicion overtook Harriet that perhaps he did, that she was part of his new life and the reason why he had disappeared. Unable to bear it, she launched herself forward yelling, 'Daddy! Daddy!' in a strange croaky voice that did not work properly, catching her toe on the edge of the pavement as she reached him and falling on hands and knees at his feet.

Strong hands lifted her and set her upright, and a man's voice spoke to her in Greek. One of her knees was bleeding. She looked up at him for the first time and a stranger looked back at her, someone who did not even look very much like her father, close to; only the colour of the hair and his shape were the same and had played a cruel trick on her. She felt her face go scarlet with shame and disappointment as she burst out, 'I thought you were my father.' He said something to his companion, who bent towards Harriet, her blue eyes friendly.

'Are you English?' she asked.

Harriet nodded.

'I speak a little,' the woman said. 'I think you have lost your father, yes?'

All at once it came to Harriet that she had indeed lost him, not just for weeks or months but forever; everyone else had been right and she wrong. He was in the beastly graveyard at home, where Ellie went to put flowers and where Harriet had refused to visit because of her belief in his living. Her heart felt as if it were cracking in half. She saw two faces, the man's and the woman's, both full of concern, through a blur of tears, and started to sob uncontrollably.

It was a subdued party that returned to the villa that evening. Harriet fell asleep with her mother's arms round her, worn out by emotional upheaval. Cleo and Luke discussed the pictures they had seen in muted tones. Cass was silent. Even Alex, who could be counted on to mention Homer's wine-dark sea on most journeys, said little as he drove through the falling dusk.

Harriet's disappearance had affected them all, but Ellie, of course, had suffered the worst. On finding that Harriet had vanished, she had searched the street where she had been shopping, forcing herself not to panic. When the search proved fruitless and language difficulties precluded asking questions of passers-by, her mind turned to the police. Feeling unequal to tackling them alone, she decided to go straight to the Café Christos, where the family was to congregate. She yearned in particular for Alex's support. In her distraught state, with her head full of visions of paedophile rings, she took several wrong turnings before eventually finding the right street and the café itself. And there, seated at a table with two charming strangers, she had found Harriet, her composure wonderfully restored by ginger beer and ice cream. The wave of anger that follows the initial relief after a bad fright was quelled in Ellie by the woman's explanation. Harriet looked at her with pleading eyes and hugged her fiercely. It was apology enough.

After the family had gathered at the café, Alex ordered wine and Ellie had given them a sketchy account of what had happened. Harriet's saviours had made a smiling departure, waving aside Ellie's heart-felt thanks. Taking Alex to be Ellie's husband, the woman touched Harriet's shoulder, saying how pleased she was that Harriet had found her father. Ellie had no alternative but to give the others the full reason for Harriet's vanishing. Shocked, they received it in virtual silence; only Cass muttered, 'I told you, she needs help.' Harriet was spared this post-mortem on her behaviour; Luke had taken her to watch a game of cricket, in progress in the nearby gardens. On the way home they dropped Cass off by Hans's apartment for her date, and as the car descended the curving coast road towards the villa, it occurred to Ellie that Philip's death had touched each of them in one way or another. What was more, its repercussions kept on coming, like the watery circles in a pond after the dropping of a stone. Harriet's fixation had a particularly painful significance; it was as though his ghost had returned to be amongst them.

'Lamb chops, sausages, chicken pieces, swordfish steaks,' Ellie counted. 'Salad, feta cheese, peaches.'

It was the end of the second week and Cass's birthday, and a barbecue on the beach was in preparation. Every workspace in the kitchen was piled with food, and Cleo was packing it into freezer bags as Ellie checked off the items. Alex came to see how they were progressing.

'All going well?' He put an arm round Ellie's shoulders and then, as an afterthought, round the shoulders of his wife. 'Luke and I have set everything up down there, and we'll start transporting the load when you're ready.'

'About five more minutes,' Ellie said.

Cleo raised her head to give him a brief smile. Her impeccable skin had acquired a satisfactory even tan which Ellie, with her blondness, could never achieve. Cleo was perfectly aware that Alex imagined himself more than a little in love with Ellie, or as Luke would have put it, 'Fancied her something rotten'. It did not disturb her; her theory being that give a man a long rein and he'll never stray far.

'What about the wine?' she asked.

'All under control,' Alex replied.

Cass would have been much happier to dispense with any kind of celebration of her birthday. She had never been socially inclined; as a child she had shrunk from children's parties, far preferring to be taken to a theatre or a film. It would have been a relief if she had been allowed to spend the evening with Hans and his crowd, having a light-hearted booze-up in a disco; a relief to get away from the claustrophobic atmosphere of family. But Ellie had been determined to do her bit as a proper mother and organize something, and to ask their limited circle of acquaintances, including Malcolm and Walter, and a couple called Talbot with a lone daughter of Harriet's age.

'You can always go on to a disco later,' Ellie had pointed out when Cass had voiced her views. She must have said something to Alex, because he took Cass on one side and delivered a short homily.

'Let Ellie do this for you,' he advised. 'It's her way of showing how she loves you. She's had a rotten year

170

and it's up to all of us to make her happy, however unimportant the issue.'

His words riled Cass. She had always been fond of Alex, but she found his attitude towards her mother difficult to swallow. What right had he to lecture her, Cass, on her behaviour, when it was easy to see he could hardly keep his hands to himself where Ellie was concerned? The incident, slight as it was, had far-reaching consequences of which Cass was unaware at the time; it fuelled her resentment. The day before her birthday, she walked along the beach to the taverna apartments and went to bed with Hans for the first time. His flatmates had taken off on an expedition and he and Cass had the place to themselves. They had rolled and thrashed about the bed in an excess of youthful energy; afterwards they lay side by side, cooling off behind drawn curtains, their skins brown against the sheet, and told each other how wonderful it had been. It had not, in fact, been that exciting in Cass's opinion, but it had liberated her and put her in a better frame of mind.

'If you had a disturbing secret which concerned someone close to you,' she asked Hans, 'would you tell them or keep quiet about it?'

He considered. 'It depends.'

'On what?'

'On how it would affect them,' he said.

'I don't know.' She thought a moment. 'It would be a shock,' she said, 'but I think it would be better in the long run.'

'Better for the someone or for you?' he asked in his careful English.

'Both.'

He turned his blond head to look at her. 'This is to do with your mother, am I right?'

'Why do you say that?'

'Because you are uneasy with each other,' he said. 'She is a lovely woman; I think you should tell her what you know. Are you pregnant?' he added.

'Shit! No!' she replied indignantly. 'But it's worse than that, even though it's in the past.'

The barbecue broke up at around midnight; it had been, so everyone agreed, an unqualified success. Malcolm and Walter had provided the equipment, and Alex and Luke had cooked by the light of a full moon and two ancient hurricane lamps. Cass had put herself in charge of the wine, topping up glasses the moment they were empty. Ellie, watching anxiously, worried that her assiduousness would result in a collection of paralytic guests, but at least Cass seemed to have thrown off any lurking mood and to be actually enjoying herself. It was a long time since Ellie had seen her laughing; it was a blessing, she told herself, that Cass had found the four friends now joking and teasing her. Luke had brought his guitar and played after they had eaten, switching the rhythm from old Beatles songs to calypso to folk music. Harriet, the upsetting experience in the town forgotten, danced barefoot in the sand, leaping up and down with Lucy Talbot, arms flailing. Later they had swum in a sea still warm from the heat of the day under a sky thick with stars. Cleo and Luke had raced each other from the shore and their laughter drifted back over the water to where Alex and Ellie were towelling themselves. For the first time since the holiday had begun, she felt both euphoric and at peace. Alex put his hands on her arms and kissed her lightly on the lips; a brotherly unimportant kiss. They had walked back to where their guests were making

172

moves to depart and Cass was urging a last glass of wine on them, pouring herself one when they refused. She turned to Ellie, grinning, her eyes bright and slightly glassy, and Ellie realized she was more than a little drunk. 'That was great,' Cass said. 'A great party.'

'As long as you enjoyed it,' Ellie said, reaching for the glass in Cass's hands. 'Darling, I think you've had enough.'

'Whoops!' Cass dodged her. 'Last one,' she told her with a giggle. 'Where's Hans? I must find Hans.'

But he was nowhere to be seen, having drifted away with the rest of the gathering; and when they had packed up the debris and wound their way up the path to the villa, there was no sign of Cass. Imagining the two to be together, Ellie was not particularly worried, and it was not until the rest of the family had gone to bed that she wandered out to the balcony to look for her book and found Cass curled up on one of the chairs; not, as might have been supposed, asleep, but gazing broodingly into the night.

After Cass had told her the truth about Philip and left her alone, Ellie stayed where she was, sitting on an upright chair at the balcony table. Her limbs felt as though they would never move again, rendered immobile by what she had just learned. The shock was as great as when she first knew of his death; possibly greater, for that had been completely out of her hands, whereas an affair with Dominic pointed to her own inadequacy. The blow was too immediate for her to think coherently; anger, revulsion and a sense of her stupidity at not guessing the truth battled for supremacy in her confused mind.

Cass had made no attempt to soften the impact of her

knowledge, coming straight to the point in two brief sentences. 'I think you should know, Pa was bisexual and Dominic was his lover.'

Ellie had stared at her, searching her face for a reason for such an outrageous statement.

'You don't know what you're saying.'

But Cass did, and had gone on to describe the night she had discovered them, in a low unemotional voice that Ellie had not recognized. And Ellie, who up until that moment had been standing, lowered herself onto a chair because her legs were giving way beneath her.

'Why did you wait until now?' she whispered. 'Why didn't you tell me at the time, when you first found out?'

'How was I to know Pa hadn't already told you?' was Cass's answer. 'For all I knew, you might both have decided to go on living a lie. And later, when I realized you knew nothing about it – from little things you said, the way you spoke about Dominic – it seemed disloyal to Pa to say anything.' She avoided Ellie's eyes. 'It was impossible to be fair to everyone,' she added.

Ellie searched her memory desperately for tell-tale signs that she might have missed during those troubled months. But all she could recall was the dreadful wall of silence that had fallen between herself and Philip, his passive resistance to any form of real communication; that and the last days of Christmas when he seemed to have found a new kind of peace.

'If only he had talked to me.'

She thought she had uttered the words in a cry of anguish, but again she had whispered. 'We could have worked something out; I would have understood.'

Cass did not reply, her very muteness casting a

doubt on Ellie's statement. Ellie felt her resentment as a tangible thing, preventing any mutual comfort between them.

'What made you choose this particular moment to tell me?' she asked.

Cass ran her fingers through her fringe in an impatient gesture. 'I didn't choose it,' she said. 'It chose me. I drank too much and that gave me the courage. I'm tired of guarding Pa's reputation on my own.'

'Oh Cass!' Ellie looked at her hopelessly. 'I wish you hadn't kept it from me. At least we could have shared it.'

'No, we couldn't,' Cass said with ruthless honesty. 'I wanted to hand the whole responsibility over to you and pretend nothing had changed between Pa and me. What had happened was your business, yours and his, part of your private lives, nothing to do with me.' She swung her legs out of the long chair and stood up abruptly. 'You were always so close; I couldn't see how you could miss what was going on under your nose. I still don't understand. It's as if you shut your mind to a problem and hope it'll go away. But it doesn't, does it?'

The unfairness of Cass's accusation was like a knife stab in Ellie's back. What had she done to turn this once-happy little girl into a malicious stranger? Then she saw Cass's face damp with tears and guessed she was unloading her own pain and guilt on to the only other person involved.

'No, you *don't* understand,' Ellie told her quietly. 'It wasn't as simple as that. You'd better go to bed, Cass; we're both too tired to make sense.'

And Cass had left, her shoulders drooping, without a hug or a kiss, merely a muttered 'Night', turning at the open French windows. 'Alex—' she began and then, thinking better of whatever she was about to add, disappeared.

There was a painful grain of truth in what Cass had said. How, after twenty-five years of marriage, could Ellie have known so little about Philip that a momentous change in him had gone unrecognized? It made a mockery of all those years of building a life together. She longed to be back in her own house, enclosed by the comforting familiarity of its four walls, and she started to cry, the tears slipping silently down her cheeks and wetting the thin stuff of her shirt.

At that moment, Alex had left Cleo reading in bed and gone to the kitchen in search of bottled water, driven by thirst and an inability to sleep with the light on. Through the open doorways he caught sight of Ellie's figure on the balcony, and knew by her bowed head that something was seriously wrong. He walked on noiseless feet to her side and put a hand on her shoulder, feeling the small jerk of surprise at his touch. 'Ellie,' he said quietly. 'What is it?' She did not reply, merely turned a face swollen with tears towards him. He realized she was past explaining; all he could do was administer silent comfort. Gently raising her from her seat he wrapped her in his arms and felt her body relax against his with a little shudder of exhaustion. They stood like that for several minutes, while he stroked her hair still damp from the sea. At last she lifted her head as if to say something, but before she could speak he had bent to kiss her; a protracted kiss in which his arms tightened round her and he could feel her hands on his back, clutching him as though drowning.

Cleo also had a clear view from the kitchen; ready

for sleep, she had come looking for Alex, who seemed to be taking a long time finding the mineral water. She saw them etched as one against the pale moonlit night and stood, transfixed in the middle of a yawn. Then, shivering with fury, she turned on her naked heel and marched back to the bedroom, where she locked the door against her husband's return.

Chapter 7

It was fortunate, from Ellie's point of view, that Charles Stormont had delayed the writing of his memoirs. She had learned about it on one of those fine October mornings, still and sunny after a misty start, that should by rights make one glad to be alive. She felt all the more guilty, as she walked to the village, that she had allowed Philip's problems to get her down. It only happened occasionally; most days she could cope with his depression. But today she found it imperative to escape for an hour on the excuse of buying a few unnecessary groceries and some writing paper, to forget temporarily how worrying life had become.

When she entered the shop, Charles Stormont was in front of the shelves of stationery, his grey hair curling over the collar of an ancient tweed jacket. The sight of his tall stooping back view was reassuring; she regarded it with affection. He had been remarkably supportive over Philip's breakdown, never prying, but lending a sympathetic ear when asked and making tentative but sensible suggestions. More than once she had called on him for advice without being disappointed. She crossed over to him now and slipped an arm through his.

'Ellie!' He squeezed her hand in greeting, studied her face. 'Not a good day?' he queried, from which she deduced that it reflected her mood.

'It could be better,' she admitted.

'Tell you what,' he lifted a box of typing paper from one of the shelves, 'I'll take you for a drink when we're finished in here.'

'Lovely, but isn't it a bit early?'

'Nonsense.'

There were only two people in the pub when they got there, both strangers sitting at the bar drinking beer. Ellie and Charles settled themselves in the inglenook. The Bugler's Arms was one of the few country pubs which had avoided modernization; it was dark and restful and smelled of hops and furniture polish. Charles took a sip of gin and tonic and said, 'I take it there are no signs of improvement where Philip is concerned?'

She shook her head. 'I don't see how there can be until he finds a new interest, and he isn't even trying. Acting was his whole life and he was brilliant. Now that it's deserted him, he's lost every scrap of self-esteem and the will to explore other avenues.' She fiddled absently with her glass. 'I'm afraid it'll just get worse; it's so bad for him doing nothing.'

'How *does* he occupy his time?'

'Goes for long walks, quite often with Cass. I'm not sure it's all that good for a fourteen-year-old to be so wrapped up in her father, either. Sometimes he'll cook supper. Otherwise he shuts himself away in his study for hours on end. He says he's writing a play, but I'm not sure I believe him.'

'Might as well give him the benefit of the doubt,' Charles commented. He looked thoughtful. 'I wonder—'

Ellie waited.

'I've had an idea,' he went on. 'It may not interest you, or Philip, which is more to the point.'

'Try me,' Ellie answered.

'D'you remember years ago my mentioning my memoirs to you? Well, at long last I've overcome my idleness and made a start on them, and it's becoming increasingly obvious I'm going to need help. An intelligent assistant who could research and edit and generally get things in order. There's a whole lot of uncollated bumf which is mounting up.' He swallowed the last of his drink and looked at her enquiringly. 'I was thinking of Philip,' he said. 'It's hardly the most exciting of jobs, but it might drag him out of his rut.'

'I think it's a wonderful offer,' she said. 'He's never done that kind of work before; I suppose he would be qualified enough for you?'

'I'm not looking for a trained secretary, just someone with common sense. Philip has a better brain than I, I have no doubt.'

'Then it's only a matter of persuading him to take it on,' she said. 'He is so unpredictable.'

'Why not put it to him and see?'

'I think', she said slowly, 'it would be better coming from you. Would you mind?'

'Of course. No problem.'

'Perhaps you'd come for a drink this evening and ask him then?'

'I shall be there.'

'Dear Charles.' She smiled at him, cautiously hopeful. 'You're a real friend.' She tapped the box of typing paper lying on the seat between them. 'Are you planning to use a typewriter for the entire book?'

'What else? Computers are beyond me and I'm too old to learn.' He made a humorous face.

'Philip has a word processor,' she told him. 'He

could put it on that for you; it would be much quicker.'

'In that case,' he remarked, 'I very much hope he agrees to join me.'

Somewhat to Ellie's surprise, Philip had accepted Charles's offer without demur. The work appealed to him; he had been considering writing his own memoirs, so he told her, and Charles's job would be like a practise run. It would still leave him time to continue working on his play.

'You didn't believe me about my writing,' he had accused Ellie, catching her sceptical expression. But he said it with a touch of amusement, the first intimation of a return to his real self.

She remembered that time as a new beginning. Charles had bought a word processor of his own and most of Philip's days were spent at the Big House, where they worked together on the book. It seemed strange at first to have him absent during the day, but also, if she were honest with herself, something of a relief. Their lives took on a routine which for weeks they had gone without, and his bouts of depression became rarer and less extreme, until finally he was able to give up his fortnightly sessions with a London therapist. It was a settled existence, far removed from the frenetic pressure of the previous one, and she wasn't sure how much Philip missed it. She herself mourned only his talent and not the hype that accompanied it. Eventually he brought the subject up one evening, after Harriet had been put to bed and while they were having a drink before supper.

'Willie Gilmour rang when you were upstairs,' he said. 'He sent his love to you.'

'Oh?' she tried to keep the apprehension out of her voice. 'What did he want?'

'He was trying to woo me back with an offer I couldn't refuse; some prestigious production or other,' he said, his tone neutral.

'What did you say?'

He smiled. 'I managed to refuse it quite easily. I thanked him for asking after my health and told him I had decided on a career change and that it would be good to see him if ever he felt like visiting us.'

'Poor Willy,' she said.

'Why "poor Willy"?'

'I was thinking what a loss you must be to him.'

'That's very flattering to me,' he replied, 'but I doubt if he'll lose any sleep over it. He handles more than enough talent to see to that.'

She went to sit beside him on the sofa and took one of his hands in hers.

'Are you sure about the decision to give it up for good?' she asked him seriously. 'You're not doing it just for me?'

He looked into her upturned face. 'I'm doing it for both of us,' he answered, 'but primarily for my own selfish reasons. I wouldn't go through the nightmare of losing my nerve again at any price. I still dream about it, wake up sweating. That part of my life is over, finished.'

'I thought it meant so much to you; there must be moments when you miss it, surely?'

She knew she was probing, but she needed to be certain he was not making a mistake.

'Like a hole in the head,' he said cheerfully. 'No, seriously, I'll tell you what I miss: that feeling when you know you've got inside a part and are playing it as faultlessly as is humanly possible. It's magic, that feeling. Perhaps you remember?'

'Darling, I never achieved it,' she said. 'Lousy actress that I was.'

'You never had the chance.' He put an arm round her and drew her close. 'You've given up a lot for me.'

'It was my decision; I don't regret the children – apart from the few occasions when I want to drown them.' She giggled.

'You know,' he said thoughtfully, 'there's quite a lot to be said for starting a new occupation in mid-life. It's a challenge. I'm serious about writing.'

'Am I allowed to read your play?' she asked.

'Let me finish it first. I'm afraid money is going to be rather tight for a while. I suppose', he added, 'I should be asking Alex for a lucrative job, rather than taking a risk.'

'You'd hate it,' she answered. 'We'll manage.'

It was following this discussion that she had decided to look for a part-time job. With Cass and Luke both at school there was no real reason why she should not work, if Betsy Groves was willing to look after Harriet. Ellie would have to pay for the extra hours, but with any luck her earnings should cover them and still leave her financially better off. There remained the problem of what to do; she was not qualified for anything except drama, and a hazy knowledge of how to work Philip's word processor would not get her very far. A desire to work with children eventually drove her to gather up her courage and make an appointment to see the Mother Superior of St Theresa's, the convent where Cass was already at school, and where Harriet would go at five years old. By a stroke of fortune an English teacher was leaving to get married, and by the end of her interview Ellie had been offered the post, taking a class of ten- and eleven-year-olds in English and drama. The fact that she had had no training did not seem to worry the Reverend Mother, who had known Ellie for some years now and preferred to have someone she could trust in charge of her pupils. Ellie started one Michaelmas term, shaky with nerves, and never looked back. She produced three shows a year, Shakespeare in the summer, and a pantomime and a Nativity play at Christmas, besides striving to fire her class's imagination with the English language. She found she had an unsuspected flair for what she was doing, and the remuneration, modest though it was, made her feel she was contributing.

'It's ages since we've seen you all.' Marge Stavely's voice came fluting down the telephone to Ellie with barely a hint of reproach.

Ellie felt immediately guilty. Contact with her in-laws had been minimal throughout her marriage. It was not her fault; Philip kicked up such a fuss whenever she suggested asking them over, she was apt to take the coward's way out and drop the subject. But she felt sorry for Marge, who adored her younger son. She could not be blamed for the mutual animosity that existed between Philip and his father.

'Why don't you come to lunch next Sunday?' Ellie heard herself say with a sinking heart.

'May we, darling? That would be lovely.'

'Oh God!' Philip groaned when she told him, raising his eyes dramatically to heaven. 'Couldn't you have thought up excuses?'

'Not for every weekend for the next six months,' she

pointed out. 'They *are* your parents, after all, and they're not getting any younger.'

'Well, let's ask Alex and Cleo to ease the strain.'

'I've already tried; they're doing something else. What about Charles? He could talk to Hugh about country pursuits like shooting.'

'I'm not having Charles bored to tears by Pa,' Philip said.

'Then I'll ask James,' Ellie said calmly. 'We haven't seen him recently.'

'James *Frobisher*?'

'Yes. He's rather good with people in a quiet sort of way, and the children like him.'

Hugh and Marge had aged noticeably, as Ellie had predicted. He had difficulty in extricating himself from behind the steering wheel of the car and walked with a stick; she had grown more fragile and brittle, as if she might easily snap in half. Only her baby-blue eyes remained remarkably youthful. It had been an early September day, still and sunny, and warm enough for them to have drinks in the walled garden. The children had hung around awkwardly, not quite sure what was expected of them and disappearing at the precise moment that Ellie wanted to dish up lunch. Everything went comparatively smoothly for the first three quarters of an hour, James primed by Ellie, had proved invaluable, and kept Hugh talking at length by encouraging the old man to recount his wartime experiences.

It was too much to hope that they could get through an entire meal with equal tranquillity, Ellie realized afterwards. Hugh's well-meaning attempts to communicate with the children resembled interrogations. Luke had won a musical scholarship to his next school and was sick with apprehension at the thought of boarding in ten days' time.

'Nothing like it,' Hugh told him. 'Teaches you to stand on your own feet. Plenty of games, too; that'll put some colour in your cheeks. Looks as if you need more exercise.'

Luke shot his grandfather a look of sheer dislike and didn't reply. Thin and pale and a replica of Philip, he was an obvious target for Hugh's contempt.

Four-year-old Harriet, propped on a cushion between Ellie and Marge, had not taken her eyes off Hugh since the beginning of lunch. She tugged at Marge's arm to attract her attention.

'I don't like Grandpa,' she announced in a sibilant whisper in her grandmother's ear.

Ellie scooped up a spoonful of potato and gravy and adroitly popped it into Harriet's mouth.

Cass alone seemed actually to enjoy her grandfather's company and kept up a steady flow of chat centred mostly on herself. But it was not long before Philip's occupation, or lack of it, came under Hugh's scrutiny. It would have been reasonable to assume that Hugh would be delighted that Philip had ended a career which his father despised, but Hugh Stavely was not a reasonable man. He managed to twist the situation to suit himself, saying, 'Can't for the life of me understand why you wanted to chuck it in at your age.'

'I didn't expect you to, Pa.' Philip's face was expressionless. 'But if I explained it to you, you wouldn't understand any better. Let's just say it was time for a change.'

'Well, it seems to me a thoroughly irresponsible decision when you're at the top of your profession,' Hugh grumbled.

'Come off it,' Philip replied. 'You've never approved of what I did.'

His father grunted. 'Maybe not, but I'm not denying you've made a success of it, such as it is. Where do you intend to find a job at forty odd?'

'I already have; I've been in work for the past eighteen months, helping a neighbour compile his memoirs. When that comes to an end, I've decided to write full time.'

'He's going to be a playwright,' Cass said with pride. 'He's nearly finished one already.'

'Christ Almighty! From one precarious project to the next.' Hugh clattered his knife and fork together in disgust.

'Please don't blaspheme, Hughie,' Marge said with surprising sharpness, 'and stop interfering; Philip's old enough to make up his own mind. I for one think it's very brave of him to start afresh,' she lifted her wine-glass to Philip, 'and I wish you all possible luck, darling.'

'Thank you, Ma.' He leaned from his chair to kiss her cheek.

It was James who had come to the rescue and defused the potentially explosive topic of conversation. Ellie had gone to the kitchen to fetch in the treacle tart, fervently hoping it would glue Hugh's dentures together for the rest of lunch. As she returned James was describing in that quiet, rather diffident manner of his, how he had lost a lucrative job in the City and had been forced to find an alternative way of earning his living.

'It was the best thing that could have happened to me,' he was saying. 'I'm more contented doing what I do now than ever before. I wouldn't go back to the rat race whatever the financial rewards.'

187

His words seemed to have a soothing effect on Hugh; his complexion faded from red to normal. He fought, however, for the last word. 'That's all very well,' he conceded grudgingly. 'But the two situations are hardly comparable. You learned a trade working with your hands, for which I imagine there's a steady demand. There's no such guarantee attached to what my son plans to do. He's relying on ideas and luck alone.'

'Our occupations aren't so very different,' James insisted. 'I fashion my product out of wood; Philip will be fashioning his out of words. And there's a demand for pretty well everything you can think of in this world.'

The afternoon had passed peacefully enough; Hugh had mercifully fallen asleep in an armchair, and Ellie and her mother-in-law had made a slow perambulation of the walled garden, discussing plants. On the front lawn James and Philip played badminton with the two older children. After tea the grandparents had left and James prepared to cycle home, the family clustering round him in the driveway. Philip thanked him for his diplomatic intervention on his behalf.

'It was no bother,' James said. 'Other people's relations are always easier to deal with than one's own.'

'I doubt there are many like my father,' Philip answered. 'It's tempting to do something scandalous enough to give him a genuine cause for complaint.' He smiled. 'One of these days, perhaps . . .'

Ellie could recall, as clearly as if it were yesterday, meeting Dominic Fraser for the first time, and her reaction: the slight tingle of distaste up and down her spine as his hand touched hers, although there was nothing wrong with his handshake. It was firm and cool, denoting confidence. In fact there was nothing distasteful about him, if appearances were to be gone by. He had the kind of even, blond good looks that a lot of people would rave over, and the fact that they did not appeal to Ellie could hardly be held against him. His clothes had a casual chic about them which suited him, and his smile had a genuine warmth. Her instant recoil was purely instinctive and quite unaccountable.

Charles had introduced them at the launch party for his recently published memoirs, held at the Savoy.

'My nephew Dominic,' Charles had explained, trying to make himself heard above the din of a hundred voices. 'I think he might be of help to Philip; we must get them together.' And then he had been claimed by his agent and led away to circulate, and Ellie was left to discover exactly where Dominic's usefulness lay. Philip had disappeared in the crowd, but Cass was with her. It was her first grown-up party and she had been persuaded out of her layers of shapeless garments into a quite presentable black frock, which she wore with an air of boredom.

'This is my daughter Cass,' Ellie said.

'Hallo, Cass. What do you do?'

'I'm still at school,' she muttered grumpily.

'Really?' Dominic feigned astonishment. 'I thought you might be at university, or possibly training to be a model.'

Cass gazed at him, the boredom wiped from her face. 'Did you?' she said, glowing from his amazing discernment.

'Are you married to Philip Stavely, by any chance?' he asked Ellie.

'Yes. D'you know him?'

'Only of him; who doesn't? I'm a great admirer.'

'He's no longer acting,' she said. 'He wants to write and has just finished a play.'

'So that's what Charles meant when he said we should meet,' Dominic remarked. 'I write film and television scripts. I'd very much like to read what he's written. D'you think that would be possible?'

'I should think he would be only too pleased,' she said, struggling with a ridiculous reluctance for Dominic Fraser to be involved in their lives, even on the periphery. Moments later they were swept apart, as so often happens at parties, and the fifteen-year-old Cass was saying, 'He's pretty dishy, isn't he?' Ellie pretended not to have heard her. She had caught sight of Philip's dark head, distinctive amongst a sea of others, and guiding Cass firmly by the arm, made her way across the room to join him.

Charles was as good as his word; two weeks later he had Dominic to stay and arranged an informal dinner party in order for him to meet Philip. Philip had worked enthusiastically on the compilation of the memoirs, and in the eighteen months that it took to complete them, Charles had grown fond of him. He saw in Dominic a chance to do Philip a favour and possibly to open up new horizons for him. In any case, he told Ellie, Dominic had a load of contacts and it was worth a try; and she had thanked him, a little too brightly, secretly wishing Philip would push his scripts through the more conventional channels of theatrical and literary agents.

The dinner party was not a complete success. Charles had invited two other couples who had no idea that Philip had retired from the stage. To them he was still a household name whom they were eager to meet, to ply him with questions about his next production and shower him with praise over the ones that had gone before. Ellie had watched him anxiously, knowing that this was the kind of situation he disliked intensely. He did well, managing to explain his interest in writing without actually admitting that his acting was a thing of the past, and diverting them with humorous and highly exaggerated anecdotes about other well-known actors. She was surprised to note a deferential expression on Dominic's face whenever his eyes were on Philip; she had thought him to be too sure of his own worth to go in for hero-worship. It was not until the very end of the evening that Philip and he had a few moments to themselves and spent the time deep in conversation. Dominic seemed to be doing most of the talking and Philip nodding in reply, their roles all at once reversed.

'God! What an evening,' Philip had said when they were in the car, Ellie driving because he claimed to be pissed. 'Why on earth did Charles ask those infuriating people? I hate being interrogated.'

'He meant well,' she reminded him. 'He was doing it all for you. What do you think of Dominic?'

'I really don't know. I only had a few minutes alone with him.'

'You must have got some sort of impression.'

He thought for a second. 'Smooth,' he said. 'A bit of a whizz-kid. But very clued-up about what he does, judging by the way he talks. Not that I'm in a fit state to judge anything,' he added with a laugh.

'Honestly, darling,' she rebuked him, 'you're supposed to be taking this introduction seriously.'

'I am, I am. He wants to read my script. I've asked

191

him for a drink before lunch tomorrow so that I can give him a copy.'

Dominic arrived the following morning in a smart little navy blue BMW which impressed Luke no end. He was relaxed and charming with the whole family, admiring the house and Ellie's choice of colour scheme. Even Harriet, who at four years old showed nymphomaniac tendencies and climbed onto his lap uninvited, did not seem to embarrass him. He left, after finishing a modest gin and tonic, with Philip's play in his briefcase and an assurance that he would be in touch shortly. Philip was immediately hit by agonies of self-doubt.

'I feel as if I've handed my baby into the care of an unknown nanny,' he told Ellie, wandering into the kitchen where she was dishing up lunch. 'I really want something to come of this, but I've no idea if I've written a whole lot of crap.'

'You haven't,' she said. 'The play's good; a little too long, perhaps, but the talent's there.' She carried a pile of plates to the table and kissed his cheek. 'I mean it,' she added.

Two days later Philip had a telephone call from Dominic. They talked for a long time and when he emerged from his study, his face was alive with barely controlled excitement. Dominic had enthused about the script and, more importantly still, he considered it would adapt easily for filming. They had arranged a meeting at his flat in London to discuss the future and a possible partnership. Philip lifted Ellie off her feet in a bear-hug, twirled her round and round and collapsed with her onto the sofa in an undignified heap, laughing.

'I'm determined to make a success of whatever

Dominic has on offer,' he said when they had recovered.

It was on the tip of her tongue to say: but you know nothing about this man, or where all this is leading you, but she bit back the words.

'It's a new beginning,' he said. 'Aren't you pleased for me?'

'Of course I am,' she answered quickly. 'Terribly pleased.'

She really must not, she warned herself, let personal antipathy for Dominic get in the way of Philip's happiness, and of her happiness as well. God forbid she should ruin his new-found confidence. He had lived most of his adult life with success; he had become so acclimatized to it that he found it difficult to manage without it.

Within the month, Philip and Dominic were working as a team. Dominic had already established himself as a screenwriter and had built up contacts on both sides of the Atlantic, but principally in America. He had reached the stage of having his work accepted on a regular basis; quite often two of his scripts would be in production at the same time, one being filmed for the cinema and the other for a television series. The films credited to him did reasonably well and he had yet to have a failure, but neither had he been responsible for a box-office hit and 'reasonably well' was not enough to satisfy his ambitions. For some time now he had been keeping his eyes open for someone with talent to work in tandem with; someone to supply new ideas and a fresh slant to the business of writing. From the moment he had read Philip's script, he knew he had found what he was looking for. Philip had the ability, his experience of filming was invaluable, and when Dominic put forward the suggestion he had been wholeheartedly in favour. Their agreement was reached in a matter of minutes and the details discussed over lunch in a small restaurant close to Dominic's flat.

The flat was their workplace; one of the larger rooms was given over to an office with all the necessary equipment: two computers, a fax, a photocopier, telephones and filing cabinets. Philip became a commuter, leaving his car at the station to catch an early train and collecting it on the evening journey home. It was his first experience of a nine-to-five job, although the hours were not so clearly defined as that. Quite often he would telephone Ellie to say that they were working on a new idea and he would be late back. She liked the sudden busyness of their lives and the sense of security it brought. As the months passed and it became apparent that the joint venture was making money, the reservations she had about Dominic were lessened to a great extent. In the beginning she had worried that there might be a dubious side to him where business matters were concerned, and that he had involved Philip in a set-up that had no hope of succeeding. But she had come to realize that whatever failings he might have, recklessness wasn't one of them; he knew exactly what he was doing and did it competently. She guessed, without being certain, that of the two men, Dominic was the better salesman and Philip supplied the imagination. However they worked it he was deeply contented and that was what mattered to Ellie.

Perhaps the only drawback was the travelling. They flew regularly to the States for negotiations, spending a fortnight at a time there before returning, but she was used to Philip's absences in the past and reconciled herself to this bit of their history repeating itself. Dominic rented a house in Beverly Hills, an economically sound move compared with staying in hotels. Philip came back with presents for the family and they would spend lazy weekends exchanging news; he describing his latest trip, and she filling him in with information about the children, who were growing up. Cass had passed her A levels and been accepted at Exeter University. Luke disliked everything about his school apart from the tuition of music. Harriet had changed from chubby toddler into a leggy seven-year-old. Occasionally they would ask Dominic to lunch on a Sunday, and Ellie would watch from the kitchen window as he and Philip strolled up and down the lawn deep in conversation, and try not to resent the intrusion. There was clearly a close harmony between the two, and she could not help feeling the odd pang of jealousy, swiftly reminding herself that this was unfair. She ought to be pleased that they got along so well together. But weekends were precious and she regarded them as exclusively hers and Philip's, the one time they had to themselves.

Life had settled into a rhythm almost mesmeric in the sense of permanence it brought. It seemed to Ellie, and for a long while there was no reason to suppose otherwise, that nothing could possibly happen to disturb it.

It was difficult, looking back, to say exactly when things had started to go wrong; the change in Philip had been gradual, like an insidious illness. But she could remember the moment she felt her first qualm; the spasm of dismay as he told her of his decision to spend most of each week in London, sharing the flat with Dominic. Up until then, if he wanted to stay overnight, he had relied on Alex and Cleo to give him a bed.

'It makes sense,' he had said. 'It means we shall be able to work late when we need to without bothering anyone. And frankly, commuting is beginning to get me down.'

'But I shall hardly see anything of you.' She was sitting at the dressing table, removing her make-up in preparation for bed, and her partially naked face had made her feel vulnerable and without bargaining powers.

'I shall still be with you for weekends; long weekends, Friday to Monday.'

'Do you really have to be away more than two nights?' she asked in what she knew was suspiciously like a whine.

'Yes, I really do. I wouldn't be planning to if it wasn't necessary.' He came to stand behind her and bent down to catch her eyes in the looking-glass. 'Try to see it my way, darling. To do the job successfully, I must be free to come and go in my own time. Is that so difficult to understand?'

'You've managed it from home so far. Why the sudden change?'

'Oh shit! I'm not going to argue,' he had said impatiently, and strode to the bathroom where she could hear him cleaning his teeth above the gushing of the taps.

She was left feeling bleak with self-pity, but she did not raise any more objections. She had to admit there was logic in his reasoning, and he had quietly gone ahead with the new arrangement. But she was not happy with it; she saw little enough of him as it was, with his frequent American trips. Somehow she resented these less than his weekly absences; it was easier to reconcile herself to being without him when they were a thousand miles apart rather than an hour's journey by rail. She missed his homecomings each evening and the familiarity of him beside her at night. There had to be a better way to manage their lives, she told herself, and after a lot of thought she came up with the idea of renting a flat in London. She could spend two nights a week there and Philip could join her; it did not matter how late, they would be together. It would have to be close to his work, of course, and she would have to come to an agreement with Betsy Groves to look after Harriet in her absence. The onus would be on Ellie to fit her London visits round her teaching, but it seemed to her worthwhile.

When she put her idea to Philip the following weekend, he stonewalled it out of hand. His reaction shocked her; always, throughout their married life, they had discussed any new project, not invariably agreeing, but at least talking it through. Now he barely listened to the details; he was adamant in his refusal to move from Dominic's flat. The arrangement was working out very well, he told her, as he had known it would. To move elsewhere would be crazy, just for the sake of a brief glimpse of her when they were both too tired to communicate.

'At least we would have the nights together,' she had said, growing desperate at his disregard for what might make her happy.

'For God's sake, we're not a honeymoon couple, Ellie,' he had replied. 'The whole point of my lodging with Dominic is the lack of distraction.'

It was the most hurtful remark he had ever made to

her; he was not as a rule an unkind man. There was a split second in which she might have hit him; her hand had tingled with the stinging slap across his face which never materialized. Instead she searched for words to match his own, managing only to sound spiteful.

'Perhaps you'd better spend the weekends with Dominic as well,' she said with quiet fury, 'since I have so little to offer.'

His face had gone blank as if an invisible shutter had been lowered, his eyes dark and opaque, so that it was impossible to tell what he was thinking. It was a look she had not seen before, but over the months to come she was to get to know it well. She had left him without another word and had gone into the garden, pausing in the hall to pull on a raincoat against the cold March wind.

Later he had apologized, putting his arms round her and admitting he had been overworking. But she sensed these excuses were merely placatory, a papering-over of something inexplicable and far more serious than a mere spat.

Gradually they made love less and less, until finally even the rare occasions had ceased. They had fallen into a routine in which he would kiss her gently before turning on his side and lying motionless. She could tell he was not sleeping by the sound of his breathing; while she too lay without moving, stiff as a plank, her heart thudding in panic at this latest deprivation and her mind a treadmill of unanswered questions. What was happing to them? What was he thinking, turned away from her and in upon himself in the darkness? Sex had been important to them both, a carefree, spontaneous act without problems. The occasional efforts she made to rouse him, winding her arms round him to draw him close to her, had met with failure; he would slowly disentangle himself, plead tiredness and apologize, as if they were strangers in bed together for the first time. She gave up trying.

She confronted him, the first of many confrontations, while she put the mashed potato onto a shepherd's pie. It was easier, she had found, to be doing something, so that she did not have to look him in the eye.

'What's wrong between us? Don't I turn you on any more?' she asked.

'It's not like that,' he replied.

'There must be a reason.'

'I can't give you one.' He walked about the kitchen, fiddling with utensils. 'I'd make love to you if I could, but I can't. I'm impotent. Don't ask me why.'

She stopped making potato whirls and laid the fork down, suddenly anxious.

'You're not ill, are you?' she asked.

'I don't believe so. Anyway, it's not an illness,' he said evasively.

'All the same, you might ask a doctor for advice,' she suggested, striving to sound casual.

'Stop pressurizing me, Ellie,' he answered irritably. 'These temporary hitches happen; it'll come right if you don't bang on about it.'

'I'm not banging on,' she snapped back. 'It's important to me; isn't it to you?'

He gave a theatrical sigh. 'All right, all right, I'll go,' he told her, avoiding her question.

But his eyes had taken on their shuttered look, and she knew he was lying and that he had no intention of seeking help, although when she asked him later, he swore he had seen someone in London and that the diagnosis was stress. It might be best if they slept in separate beds; just for a while, he had been quick to add, to take the onus off him and to give them both a good night's rest. He had moved into the dressing room and never returned; that was when she realized that she had lost him completely. It was also the moment that she had begun to suspect him of having fallen in love with someone else, wondering why it had not occurred to her before; it was such an obvious explanation. It would not be the first time he had been unfaithful to her, but the previous incidents were superficial and had not threatened to ruin their marriage.

If he was having an affair, and as time went on she became more and more convinced of it, it did not appear to be giving him much joy. He did not look well; the skin across his naturally gaunt cheekbones drawn tighter than ever and permanent worry lines between his eyes. Worst of all, he had withdrawn into himself where Ellie could not follow, and evaded discussion whenever possible. Effectively frozen out, bewildered, hurt and angry, she fought to save what had once seemed an indestructible love for each other, vacillating between pleadings for enlightenment and direct accusations. He refused to admit that there was anything to worry about. 'All marriages go through phases,' he claimed. 'They can't always be on a high.' And in answer to the question of an affair: 'There is no other woman. You're the only one and always will be,' he told her with a weariness in the tone that very nearly, but not quite, convinced her. She could not go on for ever struggling against the lack of communication. There had come a time when she stopped trying to reach him, finding it easier to adopt his attitude and retire into her own shell.

By now they were living the lives of virtual strangers; conversation was confined to polite exchanges on mundane and non-controversial subjects. The secrets and the things that were left unsaid hung over them like a pall under which they went about the business of everyday existence, working, shopping, eating, as if nothing had changed. Ellie had come to dread the weekends that she had once regarded as precious. It was a relief when Luke and Cass were at home and Philip made an effort to appear normal in front of them. He had always been good with the children and at least that part of him had not altered. He had taken to bringing work home with him and spent a lot of the weekend writing, but he seldom talked about it; whereas once he had been eager to describe the outline of a new script to her, now she had to drag information out of him. If it were not for the evidence of a healthy bank account, she would have had no idea of the partnership's success.

Her isolation was complete; she had never known the pain of extreme loneliness before and longed for someone in whom to confide. But she hesitated, aware that the situation was too nebulous to be easily explained. How could one describe the breakdown of a relationship in which there was no obvious wrongdoing? No-one would begin to understand; it would be written off with clichés: a temporary crisis, a sticky patch, just like in a thousand other marriages.

In the end, Ellie's mother Fleur and Betsy Groves had to be told simply because they both found her in tears on separate occasions. She derived a lot of comfort from each of them in their own ways and neither of them made light of her misery.

Fleur had come to stay for a few days and the joy of having her there reduced Ellie to floods over breakfast. Her mother produced a box of tissues and heard Ellie out with her usual serenity before offering advice.

'I had the same sort of problem with your father,' she had said to Ellie's surprise. 'He was having an affair with one of my friends. I threatened to leave him. It worked wonders. Luckily we made it up long before he died, otherwise I suppose I would have felt terribly guilty. You'll have to frighten Philip,' she added. 'If you make a threat, you must be prepared to carry it out.'

'Mum, how can I leave him?' Ellie protested. 'There's Harriet to think of, and my job, and Cass and Luke in the holidays. Where on earth would we go?'

'To me.'

'In a three-bedroomed flat? Mum!'

'Well, at least come and stay with Harriet for a while,' Fleur had said. 'You're badly in need of a holiday.'

And Ellie had agreed, taking Harriet out of school for a week spent in her mother's tender loving care.

Betsy's comments had been of the all-men-are-sods variety. She had come upon Ellie putting clean sheets on her bed and crying over the acres of unused space; she cried at every little thing in those days. Betsy had marched her downstairs, sat her down in the kitchen and, fetching a bottle of brandy from the drinks cupboard, poured a modest measure into a glass.

'It's only half-past eleven,' Ellie said feebly.

'Drink it,' Betsy ordered, 'and never mind the time. It'll settle your nervous system.'

Ellie's problems were no surprise to her; she would have had to be blind to miss the signs, she told Ellie, what with Philip sleeping in the dressing room and all. Her advice differed from Fleur's.

'Don't you budge from this house,' she said. 'It's your security, and why should you? It's him should go if he's cheating on you.'

'But that's just the point,' Ellie answered, 'I don't know that he's done anything wrong.'

Looking back, Ellie wished she had taken Cass into her confidence as well, realizing that, had she done so, tragedy might have been avoided. But Cass had become unapproachable since she had been at university, and Ellie had continued to pursue a policy of pretending that things had not changed between herself and Philip. Cass veered between argumentativeness and brooding silences; sometimes Ellie would catch her watching her with a look of extreme irritation and wonder what she had done to deserve such obvious disapproval. Cass's closeness to Philip remained the same, which struck Ellie as unfair in the circumstances. Then there had come the day when Cass had returned from London on a very early train and walked into the house before breakfast. Pale as a ghost, she had gone straight to her room and stayed there until evening, emerging only to drink a bowl of soup, retreating again for the rest of the following night. Her eyes had been puffy from crying and she refused to answer any of Ellie's anxious questions, beyond a muttered excuse of feeling unwell. The incident had never been explained and she had returned to

Exeter. But from then on her attitude towards Philip had been subtly different; a constraint had sprung up and she no longer dragged him out of his study to go for walks, or amused him with anecdotes of student life. Ellie had given up trying to understand Cass's behaviour, and put her mercurial mood swings down to a phase she was going through and which unfortunately was lasting rather longer than most.

Dominic's engagement came as a surprise to Ellie; Philip had said nothing about a romantic interest, and although he told her very little of what was going on, she was puzzled he had not mentioned such a major item of news. When he did tell her, she felt a sudden irrational lifting of her spirits, as if Dominic's imminent nuptials would remove an obstacle to her happiness. She had a forlorn and unvoiced hope that the newlyweds would make his flat their home, that Philip would no longer sleep where he worked, and that somehow this would bring them together again. In her heart she knew this to be a fallacy, that the abyss between them had little if anything to do with a mere change of location. She soon learned that Dominic and Clare were buying a house; the flat would remain the workplace and Philip would continue to stay there when it suited him.

Ellie found his reaction to Dominic's engagement strange. He seemed to accept it with a kind of weary cynicism, as though the subject were scarcely worth mentioning.

'I can't imagine Dominic in love,' Ellie had said. 'He's so very self-absorbed.'

'Love doesn't come into it,' Philip had answered with quiet certainty. 'It's a marriage of convenience.'

'You mean money? I wouldn't have thought that was one of Dominic's worries.'

'Children; he wants children,' Philip said in the same flat voice. 'He's chosen a brood mare.'

She had been shocked. 'That's a really bitchy remark, darling.'

He shrugged. 'It's an accurate description; I'm merely stating facts.'

'You're going to miss him,' she remarked.

'I don't understand you,' he said, staring at her.

'I mean, you've spent so much time together,' she explained quickly, feeling flustered. 'I imagine it will feel strange with him no longer sharing the flat.'

'Oh, that. It won't make a lot of difference to us,' he replied, as if the topic held no interest for him, and he had made one of his abrupt exits, saying he was going to the village and did she want anything.

She was left with the impression that he was not telling the truth, that in fact the rearrangement caused by Dominic's plans mattered to him more than he was admitting. Philip did not go to the engagement party given by Charles for his nephew at the Big House; he was in America on a lone business trip. Ellie went on her own and met Clare for the first time; a large girl with a fresh complexion and a confident manner, wearing a dress in an unbecoming shade of red. Seeing her standing beside Dominic, Ellie was struck by the incongruity of their union; his urbanity and her lack of it made it seem so wildly unlikely. They were married a month later, a register-office ceremony since neither of them was religious, and the reception was held in the ladies' side of a men's club. Philip, for reasons unknown, had refused the role of best man. Perhaps it was just as well, for by the end of the reception he was hopelessly drunk and Ellie had to ask Charles for help in getting him downstairs and into a taxi. They were staying with Alex and Cleo, and Alex had undressed his brother and put him to bed, where Philip, who had been singing the same song over and over again, fell immediately into a deep inebriated sleep.

The next day Ellie had gone back to Darlingford, and Philip, looking haggard, had returned to the flat. They hardly spoke. There were only ten days to go to Christmas, and she dreaded it and all the obligatory goodwill that it entailed.

She had not tried to understand the transformation of Philip when he arrived home, merely sending up a silent prayer of gratitude. The yawning gap between them seemed miraculously to have closed, and for the first time in two years they were at ease with each other. There was a calmness about him which she did not recognize; from the earliest days he had been volatile and unpredictable. He reminded her now of a man resting in the aftermath of a battle that had been fought and won; which she guessed was very likely the case. A private and unexplained battle of his own. But she asked no questions, frightened of breaking the fragile peace that had descended so unexpectedly and wonderfully.

Together they wrapped presents, decorated the house with holly and mistletoe, shopped for holiday provisions and put their feet up while the children overloaded the tree with traditional baubles. The lights fused and the new quiet Philip mended them, and on Christmas Eve he had gone with her to midnight mass. Glancing at him during the service, she saw his cheek-bone glistening in the candlelight as if damp from tears, but decided it was more likely to be a trick of light and shadow. In the week between Christmas and new year he had devoted himself to the children, trying to discover, without much success, what was worrying Luke, and amusing Harriet. Cass alone remained uncommunicative. He also spent a lot of time explaining to Ellie about finances and business matters, as though he were anxious for her to thoroughly understand them. She supposed he felt guilty for having neglected such things, but she would much rather they had talked of more personal aspects of their lives. 'You sound as if you might die tomorrow,' she had told him jokingly, a remark that would live with her forevermore.

The bed was still made up in the dressing room, but since he had been back he had slept beside her, without either of them commenting on it, holding her close and in silence until sleep crept up on them. They had not yet made love, but she had been willing to wait; full of a regained confidence, she was convinced that everything would come right for them. It was just a matter of time. When he told her about Charles's New Year's Day shooting party she did not at first believe him. 'But you hate shooting,' she said, watching him clean the gun which had lain, forgotten, on a rack in the tool shed.

'I do,' he had agreed, 'but Charles has been asking me to join them for years, and it seems churlish to go on refusing. Besides,' he added, 'I'm a hopeless shot; I'm unlikely to hit anything.'

On the morning of the shoot he had kissed her goodbye and walked away from her, his boots crunching on the gravel of the drive. From the window she had watched him cross the road and set off across the fields opposite in the direction of the chalk cart track. 'Take care,' had been her parting words to him; a trite phrase spoken automatically a thousand times before. She had seen the barrel of his gun glinting in the wintry sun, and then he had disappeared behind a tall hawthorn hedge and been lost from sight.

Chapter 8

In the hall of the Old Rectory, Ellie dropped the two suitcases to the floor and looked around it, peaceful and familiar and smelling faintly of woodsmoke; never had she been more glad to be home. Harriet was already halfway up the stairs, her chagrin at having her holiday curtailed forgotten for the moment.

'I'm going to see my bedroom,' she called to Ellie.

'Hey, not so fast. You can take something up with you.'

'The suitcase is too heavy,' she protested.

'Carry the beach bag with your bathing things,' Ellie said. 'I'll bring the rest later, after I've looked at the garden.'

The last of the evening sun was warming the garden walls as she wandered through, turning the brickwork a deeper shade of rose. The earlier summer flowers were over, but the roses were in their second bloom and the air was heady with the scent of stocks. She guessed that James had been at work, for there were few deadheads and nothing had died off. Lowering herself onto a stone seat, she reminded herself to telephone him to let him know she was at home, and tried to think of a plausible explanation to give him for her return a week early. Not that he would demand one, but to say nothing would seem odd. She was tempted to tell him the truth, that she had been caught by Cleo wrapped in her husband's arms, and had left Corfu under something of a cloud. Put like that, it sounded a shoddy little story; there *were* mitigating circumstances, principally her deep distress at the time; but once she started on the cause of that, it would be like peeling an onion, stripping away layer after layer until there was nothing left to reveal. The truth about Philip was too new and too shattering for her to have come to terms with, let alone to share it with anyone. She doubted very much that she ever would.

Now, sitting in her garden more than a thousand miles from the furore she had left behind her, she had a strong desire to smile. The situation in retrospect had a distinct farcical element, and although she had admittedly behaved badly, Cleo's reaction had surely been out of proportion to Ellie's rather minor crime. They had, in the end, patched things up on the surface, but the tension remained, and the thought of living under suspicion for another week appalled Ellie.

'It's not fair,' Harriet had cried; a cry to be reiterated at intervals over the next forty-eight hours.

'Cleo's not well,' was Ellie's answer. 'The less people she has to worry about, the better.'

'If she's ill, we should stay to look after her,' Harriet had persisted.

'She's got Alex.'

'Cass and Luke are staying. Why them and not us?'

'They're grown up; they can look after themselves.'

'It's not fair.'

'Fair or not, we're leaving,' Ellie had said in the kind of voice that brooked no further arguments.

The sun had left the walled garden and the air felt chilly after the warmth of the island. She rose and started to walk back to the house, absorbed in her thoughts. It had been Cass's and Luke's choice to stay behind for the rest of the holiday. Neither of them had bothered to ask her whether she minded, and for a while their lack of concern hurt her; but her feelings had toughened by now, and she had decided she could manage quite well without them. All at once she was fed up with Cass's churlishness and Luke's inability to make up his mind about a single thing. Perhaps she had spoiled them, perhaps it was just another phase; whichever, she had her own life to sort out without constantly having to worry about them.

'Ellie.'

She raised her head to see James framed in the open French windows, a smile on his face. 'James! I was going to ring you.'

'No need now,' he said, coming down the steps to meet her and kissing her on both cheeks. 'What a surprise. Harriet tells me someone's ill, is that right?'

'That story's for her benefit,' Ellie confessed. 'It's more complicated than that. It's lovely to see you. Thank you for taking care of the garden.'

'I enjoyed it. It's looking good, don't you think?'

They went into the house together and Ellie poured drinks for them both. 'I'd ask you to supper but there's nothing in the fridge except a lemon and a bit of mouldy cheddar. It'll have to be baked beans and soup for Harriet and me tonight.'

'Why don't you both come to supper with me?' he said. 'Pasta and a green salad.'

'Yes, please. It sounds wonderful,' she said gratefully.

'So, what did bring you back so soon?'

She sighed. 'Let's just say something of a misunderstanding.'

* * *

A 'misunderstanding' was putting the result of Alex's actions rather too mildly; panic followed by a furious scene between Cleo and Ellie would have been more accurate.

When Alex and Ellie had finally drawn apart from one another, they had no idea that they had been seen. He still held her lightly by the wrists, unwilling to let her go completely. 'Oh, Ellie,' he whispered.

'Don't,' she said, turning her face away.

'I'm sorry if I've upset you. I just want to say—'

'Don't,' she repeated fiercely. 'Please don't say anything. Forget it ever happened, because that's what I'm going to do.'

She had left him standing forlornly on the terrace and gone to bed, hating herself for being so brutal. She was as much to blame as he, clinging to him like a leech, grabbing at the comfort he was offering. His closeness in those dreadful minutes following Cass's revelation about Philip had been all that she could think of. Lying in bed before falling asleep from sheer exhaustion, she was ashamed of her moment of weakness; seeing it as just another example of running to Alex for help. She was not looking forward to meeting Cleo's eyes over the breakfast table, brightly oblivious to the previous night's indiscretion.

It was not until the morning that it became obvious that Cleo had observed the whole scene. Ellie found Alex, awake and unshaven, lying on the sofa in the sitting room, having been locked out of his bedroom. Cleo had refused to answer his entreaties the night before, maintaining an absolute silence.

'I don't know what the hell to do,' he said, sitting up and putting his head in his hands.

That makes two of us, Ellie told herself, her heart sinking. 'I'll make some coffee,' she said, and disappeared to the kitchen, where she thought as long and hard as her tired mind would let her. 'It's probably best if I try talking to her,' she said, returning to Alex with two cups of coffee on a tray. 'After all, I'm obviously the cause of the trouble.'

'No, you're not,' he answered, 'but you might have more success than I had; although,' he added gloomily, 'I rather doubt it. When Cleo gets in a state, she can drag it out for days.'

By the time Ellie had dressed and geared herself up to facing Cleo, she discovered it was all for nought; Cleo's bedroom door was open and she had vanished. She remained missing for most of that day, and Alex, pale with worry, had organized the family into a search party to scour the beach and the rocks and the local tavernas. The children were agog with curiosity as to what the panic was about, without getting a satisfactory answer. Having failed to find her, Alex was on the point of contacting the police when Cleo walked up the steps to the terrace where they were all sitting, wondering what to do next, she said hallo in a perfectly normal voice and announced she was going to have a shower. For timing, her entrance could not have been bettered; everyone was stunned into silence, except for Alex who had imagined every disaster from drowning to murder. 'Where the *hell* have you been?' he demanded, anger taking over from relief. Cleo ignored him and went calmly on her way; Ellie caught up with her by her bedroom.

'Cleo, may we talk, please?'

Cleo turned a blank face in her direction. 'If you like,' she said, 'although I can't think what purpose it will serve.' She glanced at her wristwatch. 'After my shower, in half an hour, say.'

When Ellie returned later, it was to find Cleo seated on the only chair and gazing pensively out of the window. She was dressed in a white shirt and pink trousers and wore dark glasses, although it was evening and the sun had already set. Ellie had the impression that the Garboesque pose was deliberate, chosen to emphasize the plight of the wronged wife.

'There you are,' Cleo said. 'Sit down, Ellie.'

Ellie looked around her. 'Where shall I—?'

'Oh, the bed will do.' Cleo waved a languid hand and fixed her with a darkened stare. 'Well?'

'I've come to apologize,' Ellie said, coming straight to the point and sitting on the extreme edge of the mattress. 'I know that what you saw last night has upset you badly, but it wasn't how it must have appeared to you.'

'And how do you imagine it appeared to me?' Cleo asked coldly. 'You and Alex were in the throes of making love, were you not?'

'Not exactly,' Ellie felt her face getting fiery. 'I had just learned something that came as a terrible shock to me; I was crying and Alex tried to comfort me. It happened on the spur of the moment; there was nothing calculated about it,' she said.

Cleo gave a short laugh. 'No? You could have fooled me.'

'If anyone was at fault, it was me. I shouldn't have allowed it to happen,' Ellie said quietly.

'No, you certainly shouldn't. Behaving like a tart with someone else's husband is a strange way of returning kindness and consideration such as you

214

have received from me. Don't you agree?'

'I agree about your kindness but not about my behaviour,' Ellie replied firmly. 'I'm truly sorry I've hurt you, Cleo. What more can I say or do?'

'Very little. The damage is done,' Cleo remarked unforgivingly, making it apparent that she was going to extract every ounce of her pound of flesh. Ellie was amazed to see her, a strict non-smoker, pick up a packet of cigarettes from the table beside her, extract one and light it with a match. 'Now I've had time to think,' she continued distantly, 'I've decided the best thing would be for me to divorce Alex, since you obviously have a fatal attraction for each other. You're welcome to him; presumably you would be willing to overlook his weaknesses.'

This statement was so blatantly rehearsed, Ellie had to smother a laugh.

'You really are getting the situation out of all proportion,' she said. 'Anyone would think that you had found us in bed together from the meal you are making of it.'

'That was where you obviously wished to be.' Cleo drew inexpertly on her cigarette and Ellie saw her hand shaking. 'I'm not blind, you know. Don't think I haven't noticed you throwing yourself at him the entire holiday.'

The gross unfairness of the accusation made Ellie catch her breath. Her efforts at reconciliation crumbled.

'That's a complete fabrication, Cleo, and you know it.'

'You're in no position—'

'No, you listen to *me* for once,' Ellie told her. 'Ever since we arrived here, you have seen to it that Alex and I were alone together on every possible occasion:

215

shopping trips, expeditions, swimming, sunbathing. Your continual cry has been, "Oh, you go with Alex, Ellie, I'm busy with this, that or the other." Or, "I want to finish my book, you keep Alex happy." Can you deny it?'

Cleo, examining her nails, was silent.

'What are you trying to prove, Cleo? That you're in control in your marriage, and whatever freedom you give Alex, you can get him back at the drop of a hat? Don't bother to answer, it's none of my business. But what I do mind is being used as bait in your experiment.' Ellie found her hands, too, were shaking, and clasped them tightly together. 'I should never have come here in the first place,' she said. 'I know you asked me out of kindness, but it was a mistake. It's best if I leave as soon as possible.'

Neither of them spoke, and for a moment the silence was absolute, so that the chorus of cicadas outside in the olive grove seemed to double its volume. When Cleo at last raised her head, there were tears on her cheeks.

'Alex has always loved you,' she said. 'Right from the start. D'you remember when we met for the first time, staying with his parents one weekend? I knew from that moment on it was you he really wanted; only that was impossible, you already had Philip.' She took off the dark glasses with a sigh and laid them on her lap. Her mascara had run, leaving smudges under each eye; they had the effect of making her seem vulnerable. 'I was jealous of you then, Ellie, and I've been jealous of you ever since. So now you know.'

Ellie listened, appalled, to the collapse of Cleo as she had known her, the confident, sophisticated, opinion-ated Cleo who never doubted her own worth, and hated herself for being the cause of it. She groped for the right words to restore at least some of Cleo's self-esteem.

'There was no need,' she said gently. 'Alex doesn't love me; it's you he loves, Cleo. He merely feels sorry for me because of Philip dying, and that's quite different.'

Cleo reached for a box of tissues and blew her nose. 'I really don't know how you can be sure *what* he feels about me,' she said pessimistically.

'From the way he talks about you, little things he's said; nice, affectionate things.'

'We've grown apart. I know I often irritate him.'

'All marriages have their good and bad moments,' Ellie insisted. 'Ours certainly did.'

Cleo looked surprised. 'Did it? I always imagined yours to be immune from the snags and pitfalls of ordinary unions,' she said with a touch of sarcasm that showed she was recovering.

'Well, you were wrong.' Ellie wondered what Cleo's reaction would be if she told her the truth about Philip, thus putting Cleo's marital problems into the shade. 'I never realized you saw me as a threat,' she said. 'I promise you I'm not.'

'It's the small things that get to one,' Cleo remarked dubiously. 'The way he looks at you, or touches your arm, teases you; things like that just don't happen between us.'

'That is only flirting,' Ellie said, 'and what man doesn't flirt? It's quite harmless, it means nothing.' She glanced at her watch. 'It's eight o'clock. Shall I do something about supper?'

'Don't bother; we'll eat at the taverna.'

Ellie rose and wandered to the window. Darkness

217

had fallen and a half-moon hung above the sea, casting its path across the water.

'It's so beautiful, this place,' she said. 'I shall miss it. Thank you for bringing us here.'

Cleo came to stand beside her. 'There's no need for you to go,' she said awkwardly, mollified by gratitude. 'We've been friends for a long time, Ellie, haven't we? It would be a pity to part with any bad feeling.'

'We won't,' Ellie answered, 'but I *shall* leave, for a different reason.' She turned to Cleo. 'I've been here for a fortnight; I think you and Alex deserve the last week to yourselves. I'll see about changing our tickets in the morning.'

'All of you?' Cleo asked in dismay. 'Won't you let Cass and Luke stay on? It would be a shame to spoil the end of their holiday.'

'Well, if you're sure they wouldn't be a bother.'

'I'd be disappointed to lose them,' Cleo said.

Forty-eight hours later Ellie and Harriet were on the flight home, having been seen off by Alex, Cass and Luke. Despite their surface reconciliation, there was no doubt that Cleo looked considerably more cheerful at Ellie's imminent departure. Ellie had not spoken to Alex alone since the night of their indiscretion; he was unusually subdued and markedly attentive to Cleo, and said goodbye to Ellie with a brief peck on the cheek.

'What's all the drama in aid of?' Luke had asked her as she did her packing. 'Have you upset Cleo?'

'Why should it be me?' she had snapped back.

Cass had said nothing, but her face spoke volumes. And well it might, Ellie told herself, for if she hadn't chosen to make Ellie unbearably miserable, the trouble with Alex would never have arisen.

*　　*　　*

Ellie had read, from time to time in newspaper and magazine articles, that it was easier for a woman to accept her husband's infidelity with a male lover rather than with another female. While she could understand the logic of this theory, she now discovered it to be a fallacy. Try as she might, she was finding it impossible to come to terms with the love that had existed between Philip and Dominic; for a very real and intense love it must have been for Philip to take his own life when it finally failed him. The fact of his bisexuality was shattering enough, but far, far worse was the knowledge that they had shared twenty-five years of married life without her being aware of it. Had she been particularly obtuse? Had there been other homosexual affairs about which she had known nothing? Or had Dominic been the one grand passion, the one deviation that had taken him without warning and set him on a course to disaster? She drove herself mad with unanswerable questions and wished fervently that her rival for Philip's love had been a woman; a straightforward situation which she could at least understand, instead of groping bewildered in the dark.

After five days of this solitary introspection, Ellie came to two decisions: she would put the house on the market – the memories had become unbearable; and since he was the only person with the answers she needed, she would ask Dominic for an hour of his time. Both these resolutions she set in motion immediately before she had the chance to change her mind. Meanwhile, Cass and Luke arrived home, staying long enough to put a load of washing in the machine before leaving again for separate destinations. Cass was going to Amsterdam to meet Hans's parents, and Luke to London and then Cornwall to spend a week with a friend. There was no chance, in the short time they were with Ellie, to tell them about the house, but she suspected the sale of it would make little difference to them now that they were leading their own lives.

She had not been prepared for the rapidity with which the estate agents worked; within days of her contacting them they were telephoning her to make appointments for prospective buyers. The Old Rectory came under the heading of desirable properties; there would be no problem, they assured her, in selling it at the asking price, the size of which took her breath away. From the moment the first couple came to view, Ellie began to regret her decision. She suggested they wander round on their own, and listened to the sound of their footsteps overhead with growing hatred and despair. She realized she had rushed into action without thinking it through or having an idea as to where she would move next. Only when she looked at the view from her bedroom window, following the line of the chalk track to where it met the woods with her eyes, did she remember the reason for this foolish step.

'You have the right to change your mind,' James reminded her, reasonably enough. 'You're not committed; you can withdraw it from the market.'

She had asked him to supper and they were sitting, coffee and brandies beside them, with the windows open to the garden. It had become the usual practice for them to have a meal together at least once a week, a satisfying arrangement into which they had slipped without actually discussing it. His reaction to the news that she was planning to leave the village had surprised her; he seemed genuinely to mind and had fallen unusually silent, putting a constraint on the evening in question. Now she was having second thoughts, she imagined she could detect a flicker of hope in his eyes.

'I'm not sure about anything at the moment,' she confessed, pushing her fingers through her hair restlessly. 'There's someone I have to talk to first, which may alter the way I feel; I'll wait and see.'

She had not told Dominic her reasons for coming, in case he refused to see her; there was a matter she wanted to discuss with him, she had explained over the telephone. A sudden spasm of nervousness hit her as she rang the doorbell of the South Kensington flat, and she had a panicky desire to run away down the stairs and into the freedom of the street. It was too late; he opened the door to her, greeted her warmly and led her through to the sitting room where he asked her what she would like to drink: coffee or something stronger. She decided on gin and tonic, and while he was fetching ice from the kitchen, she let her eyes travel round the room and tried not to think about what had taken place between Philip and Dominic in this pleasant and unassuming flat.

After he had handed her the glass and they had exchanged platitudes about his wife and her family, he remained standing, as though he could sense the tension in her manner. His blond hair was lit by the midday sun coming through the window, and she thought once more how conventionally good-looking he was. He raised his eyebrows and looked at her enquiringly.

'You wanted . . . ?' he began.

'I know about you and Philip,' she said. 'Cass told me.'

'Ah.' A very faint flush crept over his face; he lowered his eyes and gazed intently at the glass he was holding. 'I very much hoped you would never need to know,' he answered. 'It must be dreadfully hurtful.'

'It is.'

'I can understand your bitterness and anger.' He sank onto a chair opposite her. 'Ellie, if there was anything I could say or do to help, I would; but I can't. I have no defence.'

'You *don't* understand,' she said. 'I haven't come here to make a scene, to tear you apart. As to my feelings, the worst of my anger burned itself out; it won't bring Philip back, will it?' She took a sip of her drink, and then a second one, before adding, 'What I feel now is confusion. If Philip had fallen in love with a woman, there wouldn't be a problem: I'd know where I was. As it is, I'm floundering in the wilderness, and that's where you can help me.'

'I'll do my best,' he said. 'Just tell me how.'

'One question is all I really want answered.' She hesitated, searching for the right words. 'Can you imagine what it's like to live with someone for most of your adult life, and to believe that you are close as it's possible for two people to be, only to find there's a whole side to them that you never knew existed?'

He nodded slowly, waiting for her to continue.

'The shock is bad enough,' she went on, 'but there are worse aspects. All at once I've been forced to query our entire marriage, to wonder which bits of it were truly as happy as I thought they were, and which were a cover-up to hide the fact that Philip was gay. I feel a fool not to have realized; but then he professed to

222

have a down on gays, he was always on about them, to such an extent it made me cross. I suppose', she said sadly, 'it was a case of protesting too much.'

Dominic shook his head. 'So much of what you're saying is way off course, Ellie. I think I know the question you want answered. Why not go ahead and ask me?'

She drew a deep breath and looked at him; his dark-blue eyes were surprisingly compassionate. 'I'd find it more bearable if I *knew* whether Philip had homosexual affairs before – before he met you, or whether you were the one and only deviation; the one great relationship of its sort, which happened quite unexpectedly. He is far more likely to have told you than me about certain parts of his life,' she said, unable to keep her voice entirely free of bitterness.

Dominic asked, 'Is that it?'

She nodded.

'Right,' he said. 'What you have to understand for a start is that Philip was not gay. He wasn't even truly bisexual; I am, or was. He would have been perfectly content to keep the love that developed between us on a platonic basis; a kind of David and Jonathan affair. I was the instigator, the one who insisted on carrying it a stage further.' He rose to his feet abruptly and started to pace up and down, as though the memory hurt. 'It was the first time that anything of the kind had happened to him. I think the whole concept secretly horrified him, but he loved me and wanted to please me. The trouble was, he never stopped loving *you*, and the leading of a double life put an intolerable strain on him. He tried to compensate for the guilt he felt by talking about you continually, as if he were trying to demonstrate to me how important you were to him.

There was no doubt he regarded life with you as real; I was merely an addiction he couldn't shake off.'

He paused and appeared to be thinking. Ellie waited, her mind numbed by his flow of words. When he spoke again, his voice was oddly choked.

'I didn't bring him happiness,' he said. 'For a long time I refused to admit it to myself, determined not to lose him. But eventually I realized that it wasn't going to work out, ever; that in the end he would return to you completely and I would be left with a bloody awful void. That's when I decided to take the initiative and marry Clare. Part of me wanted to prove that I could achieve what Philip had: a wife and children. I was abominably selfish; I never really stopped to consider the consequences.'

He broke off and went to stand by the window with his back to Ellie. His shoulders were heaving, and when he turned to her at last, she was shocked to see he was crying, the tears streaming down his face unchecked.

'So,' he said with a travesty of a smile, 'now you know where to put the blame, Ellie; I don't know whether or not that makes it more bearable for you. I ruined both your lives and I killed Philip.'

She cried in protest. 'That's ridiculous, Dominic! No-one can be sure he even took his own life.'

'Except for you and I,' he said. 'If it weren't for me, he would be alive today; I might just as well have pulled the trigger for him.'

Faced with his misery, she wished she could show the same compassion that she had seen reflected in his eyes. But all she felt was an immense sadness for Philip, and the relief of knowing that he had never been wholly lost to her.

'You shouldn't blame yourself, Dominic,' she said. 'The final decision in all this was Philip's alone.' She got up from her chair and stood awkwardly, anxious to leave him and not knowing how to do so with suitable grace. 'I must go now,' she told him. 'I hope you will be happy with Clare. Don't let the past jeopardize your chances. And thank you for explaining to me; I'm sorry it was distressing for you, but for me it was a great help.'

They did not kiss or shake hands before she left, nor did he come to the front door to see her off. Glancing back as she let herself out, she caught a last glimpse of him in the corridor, and he lifted a hand in farewell. His shoulders drooped, giving the impression of a much older man; and it seemed to her that he had aged quite suddenly in the short time she had spent with him.

On the train going home she remembered the letters. She had imagined that Philip had kept them as a memento, a final slender link with Dominic which he could not bear to destroy. Now, in the light of all that Dominic had told her, it seemed far more likely that they had been overlooked in the midst of Philip's misery, in spite of his efforts to leave no hurtful evidence behind him. She found this new explanation greatly consoling.

Hilary was rootling around in a corner of the junk shop where an assortment of paintings were stacked against the wall. She straightened up holding a small canvas and called to Luke, who was examining a suit of armour.

'How about this?' she said.

He wandered over and stared at the head and

shoulders of a woman. The background was dark olive green and the whole canvas was badly in need of cleaning.

'I don't know,' he said dubiously. 'What's so great about it?'

'Don't you think it's like Mum?'

He looked again at the shawl flung around the shoulders and the wild dark hair. 'It's meant to be a gipsy, surely?'

'Exactly. I've always guessed Mum has Romany blood, though when I ask her, she says it's a whole lot of cock. I wonder if it's going cheap?'

Scavenging in junk shops was not what they had planned to do. The idea had been to go to Kew Gardens, see the tropical greenhouses and have a ploughman's in a nearby pub. But that morning it had been raining for the first time for weeks. Hilary had set her sights on renting a small flat of her own, and was busy collecting bits and pieces with which to furnish it. Luke was amenable to the change of plan, but after four hours of bargain hunting, he was longing for fresh air and a pint of bitter. The rain had stopped when they emerged from the last shop and the sun had come out, so they walked the short distance to a pub they both knew, tucked away behind the main drag of Notting Hill Gate. There was a garden where they found a free table, and sat with their drinks, surrounded by Hilary's purchases of the morning; the picture, a set of table-mats decorated with bird prints and a pewter vase, which he privately thought hideous.

'They're hardly essential items for furnishing a flat,' he teased her, drawing froth off his beer with a large mouthful.

'Essentials are boring,' she replied. 'I can get those any time.'

'Isn't it very expensive, renting a flat?' he asked.

'Depends where it is, obviously. There are plenty of grotty areas near the hospital, and I'll have to work in my spare time, but I do that anyway. I'd probably have to have a lodger as well, to help pay the rent.' She pushed her glasses onto her head and gave him a steady look with her amazing blue eyes. 'That's enough about me,' she said. 'Tell me about Corfu.'

'I talked about that last night,' he reminded her. 'There's nothing much to tell; sun, sea and a lot of eating and drinking sums it up.'

'You're hiding something,' she said shrewdly. 'Something happened while you were there, didn't it?'

'What makes you say that?' he asked carelessly.

'You're different; I noticed it straight away. You're more confident, like – oh! I don't know – like you've grown up.'

'So what was I before, just a kid in short pants?' he said huffily.

'I think you've met someone,' she commented. 'Am I right?'

'No, you're not. One thing's certain, *you* haven't changed; you're nosy as ever. I'm hungry,' he added. 'I'm going to get a sandwich; d'you want one?'

'Yes, please. Brown bread.'

The sandwiches were the only excuse he could think of to get away from Hilary's powers of perception. He was not really surprised that she had come uncomfortably close to the truth; the pride of achievement he felt must show, he supposed, like a kind of visible aura. He didn't want to keep what had happened to himself; he longed to shout it to the world. But for Cleo's sake

227

he knew that wasn't possible; her reputation must be protected, he told himself with a glow of righteousness. He had very nearly told Hilary when he'd arrived at the scruffy flat in Maida Vale the previous evening, but thought better of it, frightened of her reducing his precious secret to mundane fact: he had slept with his aunt. Put like that it sounded smutty, even incestuous, while in reality it had been beautiful and lyrical and romantic. It had also been totally unexpected. Cleo had suggested a late-night swim and neither Alex nor Cass had wanted to go, so it had been just the two of them who had walked down to the sea through the olive grove. After they had finished swimming, they spread their towels on the little piece of sand that was hidden by the rocks and talked for a long while. Eventually they fell silent and lay on their backs gazing up at the stars, spread so thickly above them they looked like spilled milk. He had wanted to know why his mother had gone home so suddenly, but Cleo had told him not to worry, it was just a misunderstanding, and in any case, it was all water under the bridge. Then she had leaned over and kissed him; her lips tasted of herbs and sea salt, and when she lifted her head from his, she asked him if he would like to make love. His heart had thudded and he was trembling, but the moment had passed; he stopped thinking and was conscious only of a series of sensations merging together into one momentous whole. After it was over, she had lain with her head on his chest and his arms around her, and he knew his fears of making a fool of himself had left him for ever.

'One round of prawn and lettuce, two rounds of bacon and egg,' the girl behind the bar was saying. 'You're dreaming; are you in love or what?'

Luke rummaged in his pocket for the money. 'Sorry.'

Hilary seemed to have forgotten what they had been talking about when he returned to their table; either that or she had lost interest.

'Have you decided what you're going to do?' she asked, biting into a sandwich. 'Will you be going to your college of music?'

'Yes,' he answered. 'Mum's persuaded me. I still don't know if I'm doing the right thing but there's nothing else I want to do.'

'Nothing?'

'Well, I'd quite like to be a carpenter,' he said. 'If music fails me, I might go for that.'

'Is that a hidden talent of yours?'

'I don't know about talent, but I'm interested. I've helped James in his workshop from time to time.'

'James?'

'James Frobisher. He restores antique furniture at his place in Darlingford. Mum and he are friends; I guess he's in love with her,' he added.

'Really?' Hilary grinned. 'It'd be nice if she got married again. She's probably lonely.'

After lunch Hilary had to go to work. She had a job cleaning a bachelor flat; she did not enjoy it, she told Luke, but the pay was good, and there was no-one there during the day to boss her around. Luke went back to the flat in Maida Vale and spent the rest of the afternoon reading and occasionally thinking of Hilary. He was staying with her for the two nights he was to be in London, sleeping in the bed of an absent flatmate. He had discovered that he no longer felt the urgent need to sleep with her; not because he had gone off the idea, but because he was willing to wait. There would be a right moment, Cleo had said to him, ages ago it

229

seemed now. Until then he was contented to let friendship with Hilary evolve at its own pace.

That evening they spent at home, eating a Chinese takeaway. 'Where will you live when you're at college?' she asked out of the blue.

'No idea,' he said. 'Why?'

'Well,' she dug her fork into a prawn, 'if I find a flat I'll be looking for a lodger, won't I? I'd rather have a friend than a stranger.'

'I'm not sure,' he said. 'Whatever you find, it'd be bound to be miles from the college.'

'It would be cheap, though,' she pointed out, and shrugged. 'It was just a thought.'

He watched her, her thin wrists poking out from the sleeves of an Indian cotton blouse and her hair, tucked behind her ears, streaked with natural highlights from the sun. 'I think it's a great thought,' he said. 'I really do.'

There was a strange car parked in the driveway of the Old Rectory when Ellie arrived home from her meeting with Dominic. Her mind was still on what had passed between them, and it was several seconds before she remembered that people were coming to view the house and James had offered to show them round. She felt disinclined to meet anyone and considered hiding in one of the outhouses until they had left; then, realizing that they had probably seen her taxi drive away, she reluctantly let herself in at the front door.

Dominic's account of Philip's dilemma had drained her physically and mentally; her confusion was gone and only the sadness was left, and the ability, at last, to mourn. The problem was that the recognized period of time for mourning was over, and that she would be expected to be recovering in the eyes of those who knew her, not giving way to a sudden and inexplicable show of grief. Few people would understand, and to explain would mean giving away Philip's secret, which she could not bring herself to do. She recalled Dominic as she had left him and was able to pity him: his, too, had to be a solitary grieving. A better person than I, she told herself, would have made some gesture of comfort and forgiveness towards him; put her arms around him, or taken his hands in hers.

From the hall she could hear footsteps tramping from room to room overhead; a woman's voice, clear and penetrating, and a deeper male one droning in reply, grated on Ellie's ears. She walked through to the kitchen and switched on the kettle for a cup of tea, hoping fervently that they had already seen the ground floor and she would be left in peace. By the time the tea was made, the voices had grown louder as they reached the stairs and started to descend them, and the conversation became audible. The woman was talking about knocking two of the smaller bedrooms into one, and adding a bathroom.

'It *could* be lovely. Of course, it's badly in need of redecoration,' she remarked in cut-glass accents.

'Patronizing bitch,' Ellie muttered to herself.

'We can make an offer,' the man replied.

James's voice could be heard for the first time. 'I don't think you'll find the owner will come down in price.' He sounded very sure of this fact.

Ellie thought they would never go, but at last the front door shut behind them and there was the slamming of a car door and the crunch of wheels on gravel as they drove away. James came to meet her as she emerged from the kitchen, mopping his forehead with a handkerchief.

'I wondered where you were hiding,' he said, kissing her.

'Sorry to desert you; I just couldn't face them.'

'I don't blame you. They were dreadful.'

'They sounded it. Thank you for standing in for me. Shall I make you some tea?'

'Please. I don't think you'd like the thought of them living here,' he said.

'I'm certain I wouldn't,' she answered. 'But then, I dislike the idea of anyone taking my place.' She handed him a mug. 'Let's take this into the garden.'

They sat on the stone seat and he asked her about her day, forcing her to invent various trivial things that she had done. She leaned back against the wall behind her, feeling suddenly immensely weary and unable to concentrate. She wanted his company and yet could not respond to it, and there was a heaviness inside her, like a constriction that she knew was sorrow fighting to escape. He put a hand over hers lying in her lap, and his face when she glanced at him was full of concern.

'Something's wrong, isn't it?' he said. 'Do you want to talk about it?'

She smiled. 'It's nothing. I'm tired, that's all.'

He rose to his feet. 'I'll leave you to have a rest now and I'll see you for supper later.'

'James?'

'Yes?'

'Would you mind very much if I didn't come to you for supper this evening? I really do feel whacked out and I'd like an early night.'

'Of course not,' he said, not quite managing to hide

his disappointment. 'We'll postpone it until tomorrow, if you'd like that.'

They walked back to the house together and he retrieved his bicycle from the garage.

'Call me if you change your mind,' he told her as he was leaving.

After he had gone, she went upstairs to her bedroom to stand by the window and gaze at the memory-haunted view, in an attempt to induce the final dam of grief to burst.

That evening James was attacked by uneasiness; from the moment he got home he found himself unable to settle. Ellie had worried him; something was obviously the matter, and equally obviously she did not want him with her, so that there was nothing positive he could do about it. He thought of telephoning her just to make sure she was all right, but decided against it in case such a move appeared intrusive. Nothing he started to do held his interest; he tried in turn television, reading, preparing himself supper and sketching a rough design for a small chair he intended to make. Eventually he made a sandwich, poured himself a drink, the second of the evening, and carried them both to the barn to see if the workshop would have its usual calming effect on him. It was dusk as he walked through the meadow and the nocturnal rustlings of small creatures could be heard in the grass on either side of the path.

He stayed in the barn for an hour, putting the final polish to a walnut bureau; an undemanding job that allowed his mind to wander back to Ellie at will. As he neared the cottage on his return he could hear the telephone ringing, and ran the last few yards, knowing it was her, almost dropping the instrument in his anxiety to reach it before she rang off.

Curiously enough, it was an old movie on television that triggered Ellie's tears, the storyline of which had nothing remotely tragic about it. Ever since James had left she had remained dry-eyed, although she longed to weep. She had had a warm bath and heated up some soup, making herself finish a bowl of it simply because she had missed lunch. And then she had started to watch the movie at random, not bothering about selecting an alternative, glad to be even mildly distracted. It had an old-fashioned happy ending, the lovers clasped in a decorous embrace. Ellie started to cry, the tears pouring silently down her cheeks and dripping unchecked onto her dressing gown, and having started, she found she could not stop. Blindly she switched off the television, and groping her way upstairs, threw herself down on her bed in a paroxysm of grief. She wept now in noisy sobs that racked her entire body; weeping for all those things so far unmourned: for wasted lives and words left unsaid and the sunshine days of happiness now past and gone. She cried until she could cry no more, and lay for a long time without moving, her face pressed against the damp patch on the bed cover.

When at last she rolled over onto her back the room was in darkness; listening, she became aware of the creaks and groans, the sounds of an old house stretching itself at night, which were never apparent in daylight. As a rule it did not worry her, she was used to it; but in her present state of vulnerability, the noises were easily translated into footsteps on the stairs. She felt acutely alone without Harriet, who was staying with Flora; alone and lonely, not at all the same thing. There was no substitute for another human being when it came to solace. She ached to be held close by someone who cared what became of her; the last time she had known such a luxury seemed so long ago she could scarcely remember. It was as she was about to fall into a well of self-pity that she realized none of this agonizing was necessary; the answer was staring her in the face, and had been for weeks, had she but given it an ounce of thought or sensitivity. Poor James; always there for her, quietly waiting and never demanding, while she had taken him for granted. Only tonight of all nights, when she needed him most, she had sent him home in a moment of blind stupidity. The hurt had shown in his expression and she had ignored it. Very likely it was too late, she had wounded him once too often; the desire to talk to him became immensely important. She struggled upright and pulled the telephone on the bedside table towards her and dialled his number by the light of the lamp, her hand shaking. It seemed to ring for ever before she heard his voice speaking her name.

'Ellie?'

'Please come,' she said. 'I need you.'

He left the house early in the morning for the sake of propriety. She watched him go from the open front door, lifting her hand in farewell as he drove away; content in the knowledge that she would see him again that evening and for many more to come.

'I'd better be gone before Betsy arrives,' he had said. 'She might not approve.'

'I doubt it,' Ellie said. 'Nothing shocks Betsy. Anyway, she'll have to know some time; that is, if we are going to make a habit of this. We are, aren't we?' she asked him anxiously.

He had kissed her in answer, smoothing her hair away from her forehead and holding her face between his hands, just as he had done the previous night when she had let him in. There had been no need to talk, although later, as they lay side by side, she had told him about Philip and Dominic. Even then he had said little, demonstrating his feelings in actions rather than words. Waking at six o'clock, she had propped herself on one elbow and gazed down on him as he slept, his blond head on the pillow where once Philip's dark one had lain. She felt no remorse or shame; it had seemed right that James should be there, filling the void that Philip had left and detracting nothing from her memories of him.

Alone once more in her bedroom, she pulled back the curtains on another still summer day. Mist had not yet cleared from the low ground; rising out of it, the hill and the wood and the chalk track were in sunlight. The view no longer held the same horrors for her. One day soon, she told herself, I shall walk up there; James and I will go together – and she threw open the window to let in the fresh air.

'You mean to say you put the house on the market without telling us?' Cass demanded indignantly.

She had arrived back from Amsterdam and Ellie had gone to meet her flight.

'You weren't there,' Ellie reminded her reasonably. 'In any case, I didn't think you or Luke would care very much.'

'Of course we care. It's home; wc've lived there all our lives.'

'I realize that, but you're grown up; and your lives have naturally changed. You're hardly ever there.'

'That's not the point,' Cass insisted. 'Everyone needs a base. Where will you go if you sell it?'

'I'm not going anywhere,' Ellie said, who had rather enjoyed teasing her daughter. 'I've withdrawn it from the market.'

'So now she tells me,' Cass muttered crossly to herself. After a short pause she asked, 'What made you change your mind?'

Ellie waited to answer while she overtook a lorry. 'I found, quite suddenly, that I had a very good reason for staying on,' she said eventually.

'I can understand that,' she said. 'You couldn't bear to leave the house after all. Memories and so on; I suppose that was it, wasn't it?'

'No,' Ellie told her firmly. 'If you want to know, it was James.'

'James?'

'I don't expect you'll approve, but that can't be helped, I'm afraid.'

'Well, you're wrong,' Cass said. 'I'm glad.'

'You are?'

'Yes. It's time you got yourself a real life, Mum. I'm glad but not surprised,' Cass added. 'It was obvious which way things were heading for both of you.'

'How interesting,' Ellie retorted with some asperity, 'since I didn't realize myself until a few days ago.'

'No, but then you never were very observant,' Cass said, quite gently for her. 'I'm sorry I told you about Pa; it wasn't fair of me.'

'Perhaps it wasn't, but it was better I should know.' Ellie was touched; apologies from Cass were rare. 'Congratulations on your First, by the way, darling; I'm

237

so pleased for you. I suppose you'll get some high-powered job in Brussels and I shan't see much of you from now on?'

'I wouldn't bank on it,' Cass replied.

Ellie finished gathering the mixed bunch of garden flowers to put on Philip's grave and took them into the kitchen to wrap them loosely in paper. She had been up to London for the day to keep a dentist's appointment and to have lunch with Alex and Cleo, and the garden smelled sweet after the airlessness of the city streets. It was the first time she had seen Alex and Cleo since the disastrous ending to her holiday and she expected it to be a strain, but as it turned out she need not have worried. They behaved as though nothing untoward had happened; Alex was his original, affectionate, avuncular self, and Cleo, for some reason, had never looked better, her perfect skin glowing. Ellie, who was taking no chances, had refused Alex's offer of a lift to the station and escaped in a taxi.

When she had wrapped the flowers, she called to Harriet, who was riding her bicycle on the front lawn. Reluctantly, Harriet dismounted.

'Do I have to come?' she asked.

'Yes, you do. Betsy's gone home and I can't leave you here alone.' Ellie guided her in the direction of the car. 'You don't have to go into the churchyard,' she said. 'You can wait for me at the gate like you always do.'

The gate to the churchyard was the furthest Harriet would go whenever it was necessary for her to accompany Ellie. Her phobia about Philip's death persisted; she no longer believed him to be alive, but the alternative frightened her, and the grave and the headstone were dreaded symbols of it. Ellie, knowing the fear to be real, did not try to persuade her. She chatted about mundane things as they drove through the village, silly little details about her day in London. Harriet, holding the flowers in her lap, stared out of the window.

The last of the sun was fading as Ellie left Harriet sitting on the wooden seat by the gate. She was halfway along the gravel path when Harriet called out to her to wait and came running towards her. 'I'm coming too,' she said.

'Do you really want to?' Ellie asked.

Harriet's jaw set firmly, making her suddenly uncannily like Philip. 'Yes, I do. Can I put the flowers in the vase?'

'Of course. First we have to fill it with water from the tap near the gate. You can do that as well.'

Harriet frowned in thought. 'D'you think Daddy knows about all the trouble we're taking?' she asked doubtfully.

Ellie sighed. 'I don't know,' she answered. 'But it's worth a chance in my opinion.'

THE END

A SELECTED LIST OF FINE WRITING
AVAILABLE FROM BLACK SWAN

☐ 99630 0	**MUDDY WATERS**	*Judy Astley*	£6.99
☐ 99618 1	**BEHIND THE SCENES AT THE MUSEUM**	*Kate Atkinson*	£6.99
☐ 99648 3	**TOUCH AND GO**	*Elizabeth Berridge*	£5.99
☐ 99687 4	**THE PURVEYOR OF ENCHANTMENT**	*Marika Cobbold*	£6.99
☐ 99622 X	**THE GOLDEN YEAR**	*Elizabeth Falconer*	£6.99
☐ 99657 2	**PERFECT MERINGUES**	*Laurie Graham*	£6.99
☐ 99611 4	**THE COURTYARD IN AUGUST**	*Janette Griffiths*	£6.99
☐ 99724 2	**STILL LIFE ON SAND**	*Karen Hayes*	£6.99
☐ 99688 2	**HOLY ASPIC**	*Joan Marysmith*	£5.99
☐ 99711 0	**THE VILLA MARINI**	*Gloria Montero*	£6.99
☐ 99696 3	**THE VISITATION**	*Sue Reidy*	£5.99
☐ 99747 1	**M FOR MOTHER**	*Majorie Riddell*	£6.99
☐ 99608 4	**LAURIE AND CLAIRE**	*Kathleen Rowntree*	£6.99
☐ 99672 6	**A WING AND A PRAYER**	*Mary Selby*	£6.99
☐ 99529 0	**OUT OF THE SHADOWS**	*Titia Sutherland*	£5.99
☐ 99460 X	**THE FIFTH SUMMER**	*Titia Sutherland*	£6.99
☐ 99574 6	**ACCOMPLICE OF LOVE**	*Titia Sutherland*	£6.99
☐ 99620 3	**RUNNING AWAY**	*Titia Sutherland*	£6.99
☐ 99650 5	**A FRIEND OF THE FAMILY**	*Titia Sutherland*	£6.99
☐ 99130 9	**NOAH'S ARK**	*Barbara Trapido*	£6.99
☐ 99700 5	**NEXT OF KIN**	*Joanna Trollope*	£6.99
☐ 99655 6	**GOLDENGROVE UNLEAVING**	*Jill Paton Walsh*	£6.99
☐ 99673 4	**DINA'S BOOK**	*Herbjørg Wassmo*	£6.99
☐ 99592 4	**AN IMAGINATIVE EXPERIENCE**	*Mary Wesley*	£5.99
☐ 99642 4	**SWIMMING POOL SUNDAY**	*Madeleine Wickham*	£6.99
☐ 99591 6	**A MISLAID MAGIC**	*Joyce Windsor*	£6.99